DEADLY EVER AFTER

Also by Joanne Pence

The Cook and Inspector Mysteries

DEATH ON A SILVER PLATTER - A QUICHE BEFORE DYING - THE MARINARA MURDERS - CLOSE ENCOUNTERS OF THE DEADLY KIND - DEATH BY DEVIL'S FOOD - BLIND DATE'S BITTER END - THE TAVERNA AFFAIR - THE MUSIC BOX MYSTERY - TRUFFLES TO DIE FOR - COOKING SPIRITS - ADD A PINCH OF MURDER - SALSA & SECRETS

The Rebecca Mayfield Mysteries

ONE O'CLOCK HUSTLE - TWO O'CLOCK HEIST

THREE O'CLOCK SÉANCE - FOUR O'CLOCK SIZZLE

FIVE O'CLOCK TWIST - SIX O'CLOCK SILENCE

SEVEN O'CLOCK TARGET - EIGHT O'CLOCK SPLIT

NINE O'CLOCK RETREAT - THE 13th SANTA (Novella)

Ancient Secrets Series (author J.M. Pence)

ANCIENT ECHOES - ANCIENT SHADOWS

ANCIENT ILLUSIONS - ANCIENT DECEPTIONS

ANCIENT PASSAGES

The Donnelly Cabin Inn Novels

IF I LOVED YOU - THIS CAN'T BE LOVE - SENTIMENTAL JOURNEY - A CERTAIN SMILE - TIME AFTER TIME

Others

SEEMS LIKE OLD TIMES - DANGEROUS JOURNEY

DANCE WITH A GUNFIGHTER - THE DRAGON'S LADY

THE GHOST OF SQUIRE HOUSE

DEADLY EVER AFTER

THE COOK AND INSPECTOR MYSTERIES
BOOK 13

JOANNE PENCE

QUAIL HILL PUBLISHING, LLC

Quail Hill Publishing

Eagle, ID 83616

Visit our website at www.quailhillpublishing.net

First edition Quail Hill Publishing ebook: August 2018

Second edition Quail Hill Publishing ebook: October 2025

First edition Quail Hill Publishing Paperback: August 2018

Second edition Quail Hill Publishing Paperback: October 2025

DEADLY EVER AFTER

CHAPTER 1

onday, 10 a.m. – 5 days, 5 hours before the wedding

Homicide Inspector Paavo Smith hated to admit it, but when the dispatcher's call came in, a stunning sense of relief washed over him. Not relief that someone was dead—he'd seen enough bodies to last a lifetime— but relief that he had something to think about besides the fact that this Saturday, in front of family, friends, and God, he was supposed to say, "*I do.*"

Angie Amalfi, normally his bright, warm, and sometimes exasperating fiancée, had turned into a one-woman wedding SWAT team. She obsessed over every detail, as if one mismatched flower petal might bring down civilization. He'd once foolishly suggested that the freshness of the sugar-coated almonds in something called a *bomboniera*—a word that still sounded like an exotic disease—wasn't a matter of life and death. Angie nearly took his head off. Since then, he'd kept his mouth shut.

If he ever imagined this new version of Angie wasn't caused by pre-wedding jitters, he'd be catching the next flight to Timbuktu.

Inspector Toshiro Yoshiwara, his partner, now steered their

unmarked car onto Geary Street. "Yosh," as he was called, had become Paavo's partner some time earlier after transferring to San Francisco from Seattle a short while after Paavo's former partner had been murdered. Yosh was large for a Japanese, tall, with broad shoulders, a massive chest, and a head that seemed a little small for all that body. He wore his hair in a short buzz cut and looked like he could split a house in two and not raise a sweat. He was also the extrovert to Paavo's introvert. He shook hands, shot the bull, and easily conversed with people, winning their confidence and getting them at ease enough to talk. He could work a room in a way Paavo had never seen before, and—to use one of Yosh's favorite phrases—people "ate it up like a Hershey bar."

Police cruisers and the Medical Examiner's van crowded the curb in front of the address dispatch had given them. Paavo's stomach sank when he saw the sign: Forever After Bridal Boutique.

He groaned inwardly. The universe wasn't just laughing at him. It was pointing and rolling on the floor.

They ditched the car in a loading zone—legitimate parking spaces had gone the way of the dodo bird in most of San Francisco—and hurried inside. The Crime Scene tech handed them booties. Yosh went straight to the body, but Paavo, as always, scanned the room first.

Wedding gowns covered headless mannequins and lined the racks, pale shapes floating in the fluorescent light like ghosts waiting their turn. The air held a faint, powdery scent. For a moment, Paavo almost expected Angie to pop out, to do list in hand. Instead, all he saw was a shrouded female form lying on the floor, blood beneath her head.

The first responding officer explained: the owner, Lillian Kobayashi, hadn't gone home last night. Sometimes she stayed late, working through the night to fix a bride's gown before the big day. That morning, her roommate, Tasha Camp, showed up with coffee.

To Ms. Camp's surprise, she found the front door was unlocked and the lights still on. It scared her, but she continued inside. In the back of the store, she found Lillian's body.

Paavo joined Medical Examiner Evelyn Ramirez crouched over the victim. She looked up with a smirk. "Well, if it isn't the happy bridegroom."

"I don't know about happy," Paavo muttered. "At this point, I just want the wedding circus over with."

Ramirez smirked. "Okay, I imagine this isn't where you want to be on your wedding week, so I'll get right down to business." She shifted back to the corpse. "As for this poor woman—one devastating blow to the head. Hard enough to crack her skull. I'd bet a hammer. No defensive wounds. Whoever did it came from behind. No warning. Just … lights out."

Paavo glanced at the pale silk gowns swaying slightly on their racks, as if they'd witnessed it. He exhaled slowly. "Time of death?"

"Over twelve hours. Store closed at six last night, normally opens at ten. Body was found at nine this morning. I'll know for sure after the autopsy, but my money says right around closing time last night is a safe bet."

"So maybe her last customer," Paavo said.

"Could be. Brides can be … temperamental."

"Don't remind me." He grimaced. "I'll check for cameras."

The shop had only one, aimed at the register.

"She never thought she needed more," Tasha Camp told Paavo. She had been asked to wait by the register in case the detectives had questions. Her hands trembled around her coffee cup. "It's a bridal shop. Who'd want to hurt her? It doesn't make sense."

"The register's empty," Yosh said from behind the counter.

"It always is. It's more for show than anything. Lillian kept a little cash in her purse in case she needed some. But almost no one pays cash in a shop like this."

"Does anything look off to you?" Paavo asked.

Tasha scanned the boutique. Her gaze slid past the racks, the silk, the veils, then snagged on the window display. She froze.

"Wait." Her voice dropped. "I need to go outside."

Paavo and Yosh followed her as she went out and faced the storefront window. Two gowns hung in place. Two more were artfully draped across chairs.

Tasha pressed a hand to the glass. "There should be three dresses hanging. Always three. Lillian would never use only four dresses." She looked up at the two inspectors. "She was half Japanese, and in Japan 'four' has the same sound as the word for death, so no bridal shop would use four of anything. One gown is missing. A very beautiful one."

Paavo felt a sudden chill. A missing bridal gown didn't just mean theft. In this setting—blood and silk and silence—it felt like something much more serious.

———

Angelina Amalfi felt as if she were walking on air as she entered the ballroom of La Belle Maison, the premier wedding reception venue in San Francisco. Once a mansion located partway up the northeast slope of Telegraph Hill, the home had been renovated some years earlier into an elegant events center. While the main floor held a reception area with sofas and arm chairs, a commercial kitchen, and staff offices, the entire upper floor had been converted into an opulent ballroom with crystal chandeliers and gold sconces.

Picture windows faced east, commanding a view of San Francisco Bay and the Bay Bridge. White cloth-covered tables circled the dance floor.

It was Monday afternoon, and that coming Saturday, Angie's

long-awaited wedding would take place—the date that she and everyone who knew her had come to think of as her Big Day.

With Angie was Sally Lankowitz, La Belle Maison's events coordinator. She had the privilege—her word—to see to it that the wedding reception went exactly the way Angie hoped it would, from the meal to the placement of the wedding cake, to the band, the music, the dancing, the photographers, and the timing of each important step along the way. Sally was a pleasant woman with over-sized red-framed glasses that perched on a stubby nose and covered a round, ruddy-cheeked face. Her brown hair was short and curly, and she wore a simple cotton print dress with sensibly short, squat heels. And no wedding ring.

Angie had toured the facility and met with Sally a few months earlier when she first contracted with La Belle Maison to hold her wedding reception. But now everything felt more *real,* as if it were actually going to happen.

Her Big Day was unimaginably close.

"This room is going to look simply beautiful," Sally gushed, holding her arms out, hands raised as she walked to the center of the large space and turned all the way around. Angie's eyes followed where Sally's hands led. "I do love the soft rose color you chose. It's so feminine, it will make you stand out even more with your dark hair and snow white dress. You'll be like a china doll."

"Thank you." Angie guessed that was a compliment. She was short, only five-two, and being likened to any kind of "doll" didn't sit well.

"Now," Sally said, with a momentary clasping of her hands, "let's talk about your wedding cake. I'm sure it will be gorgeous, so I suggest that you—"

"There you are!" A woman's harsh, shrill voice called.

Angie turned to see a young woman storming towards them. She was tall, with long, wavy blond hair, and wore a tight black suit with a short skirt. The heels on her black shoes were at least four-inches high.

Angie stood a little straighter.

"Oh, Ms. Redmun," Sally said. She didn't sound happy. "I don't believe we have an appointment."

"I don't need an appointment for this. I only have a couple of quick issues." Ms. Redmun flicked a lock of highlighted dirty blonde hair off her brow as she glanced at Angie. She was attractive and appeared to be in her mid-to-late twenties. "Do you work here as well?"

"No," Angie said. "My wedding reception will be held here Saturday."

"Oh. Nice." Her tone was dismissive. "My *entire* wedding will be held here Wednesday evening. An evening soiree will allow us to use the deck as long as Ms. Officious here"—she waggled her thumb at Sally—"can understand my simple request."

Sally looked taken aback. "Excuse me—"

"Wednesday?" Angie asked. "Your wedding is on a Wednesday?"

"Yes, because—"

Sally interrupted. "Let me introduce the two of you. Angie Amalfi, Taylor Redmun. Now, Taylor, I'll be finished helping Angie in just a bit. She does, after all, have an appointment. If you'd like to wait in the *waiting* room, Laurie will get you some coffee." Angie's antennae rose even higher. Sally had always been cloyingly courteous to her.

"No need. I'll just wait here." Taylor folded her arms and glared at them both.

Sally again faced Angie. "As I was saying, you probably want to have your cake on the east side of the room. From the windows, there's a beautiful view of the bay which makes a lovely backdrop for photos of the cake cutting ceremony."

"I see," Angie murmured. She wanted to pinch herself that

soon she would actually be the bride cutting a wedding cake. "That sounds lovely."

"I'm having mine put on the west wall," Taylor loudly announced. "How good can any photos be with glare from the windows ruining everything? I've learned from my camera people in Hollywood that that's a no-no. I mean, really."

Her words caught Sally's attention. "I don't believe we have the furniture set-up for your wedding marked that way."

"I know." Taylor strolled closer to Sally, hands on hips. She abruptly turned her back on the events coordinator and perused the room but continued to speak. "It's one of the few little things I wanted to tell you. In fact, I have no idea why any bride would want to have her cake on the east wall. The more I thought about it, the more I knew you were wrong to suggest it."

Sally's cheeks turned red. "I see, well, we'll discuss it later." As she glanced at Angie, her brown eyes seemed smaller than ever behind her large eyeglass frames. "Now, Angie, where were we? The cake, there, by the windows?"

"Well," Angie murmured. "Maybe by that west wall is a better idea."

"The glare has never been a problem, I assure you. The west side of the room has the staircase. The cake makes a much better presentation as the guests come up the stairs if it's at the opposite end of the space," Sally said, her voice getting higher with each word.

"What's more important?" Taylor asked. "A moment's presentation or a lifetime of great photographs? Also, I want my DJ to be on the south wall. No sense him being on the east and blocking the view from the windows."

"But the plumbing for the ice machine and refrigeration for the wet bar are on that wall," Sally said.

"Don't be ridiculous." Taylor all but sneered at Sally. "I'd like the wet bar on the north wall, and my DJ, who will be playing my *personal* playlist, over there on the south."

Sally looked increasingly distraught. "The wires for the speakers are on the east wall."

"I wonder if I want my band in front of the windows," Angie murmured.

Sally twirled her way. "But as I was saying, the wires—"

Taylor glared at her, lips pursed. "For crying out loud. Bar on north, DJ on the south, cake on the west. Sheesh." She tucked a lock of hair behind her ear. Her hair was thick, long and stylishly wavy, falling well below her shoulders. "It's hardly brain surgery!"

"I wonder if that would work out better," Angie said, fingers to chin.

Sally, her face pinched and tight, turned to Angie. "Only if you want your wet bar to have no ice or refrigeration, the wires for the speakers going across the middle of the dance floor, and your cake shoved in a space where people entering the reception are milling around and it will hardly be seen."

"I don't have a band!" Taylor harrumphed. "You know that!"

"I was talking to Miss Amalfi." Sally sounded more desperate with each word.

"Why would you be talking to *her*?" Taylor cocked an eyebrow. "I'm telling you what I want for my reception, and she's just standing there looking like a potted plant."

"A potted plant?" Angie gasped. "I'm the one with the appointment! Who do you think you are, taking over my reception planning?"

"Well, for one thing, you've got the whole rest of the week. I only have two days, and this so-called wedding 'assistant' has been anything but helpful. I have to do all the thinking myself."

"I'm sorry, Taylor." Sally looked on the verge of tears. "I'm trying to help you, but you keep making changes."

"I do not make changes on a whim. I come up with enhancements—to do the job, in other words, that you aren't capable of doing!"

Sally gaped, speechless, tears welling in her eyes.

Angie spun towards Taylor. "Will you *please* butt out? You're doing nothing but upsetting Sally, confusing me, and mucking up this entire process."

Taylor loomed over her. "Why are you so pushy? I've only got a couple of changes and then I'm out of here!"

Angie put her hands on her hips. "I'm pushy? I don't think so. If you'd kept your bossy-pants mouth shut, I would have been finished by now."

"Bossy-pants? What kind of infantile word is that?"

"If you prefer a more adult word that starts with a 'b,' I'll certainly use it," Angie said.

"Sally, I demand you do something about this creature," Taylor said. "Do I need to remind you how important I am? I don't have time for this."

Angie was not a violent person, but it was all she could do not to slap the woman. "Important in your own mind, maybe. But sure as hell not in anyone else's."

Taylor raised her chin. "I'll have you know, I'm going to be in a movie."

"What movie? *Bridezilla*?"

"Why you little slut!"

"Stop!" Sally screamed. "I can't take it anymore! I can't take the orders, the bickering, the mind changing, the disappointment. The fact that not one of you … you *brides* … ever thinks about me." She burst into tears. "I'm here trying to help, and all I get is criticism. You horrible, wretched creatures make me sick. Every last self-centered one of you!"

With that, she turned and ran from the room, leaving Angie and Taylor both slack-jawed in the large empty space.

CHAPTER 2

onday, 8 p.m. – 4 days, 19 hours before the wedding.
"Look, sweetheart! I found a wedding dress for you. The perfect one. I know you'll love it." He held the gown up in front of him, the satin catching the dim light in pearly ripples. "One of the most expensive in the shop, you know."

He hesitated, almost sheepishly. "It was the display model. I asked the salesgirl if she had another, but she said it would have to be ordered. I told her not to bother. I knew this one would fit—considering how much weight you've lost."

His eyes softened as they fell on the figure waiting on the bed. "My bride," he whispered. "Beautiful. You're everything a bride should be."

He set the gown gently across a chair and went to her side. "Let me help you. All those tiny buttons—impossible for you to manage in your condition. But that's why I'm here. I'll always be here."

With tender precision, he rolled her slightly, working at the row of buttons down the back of her old gown. Once, months ago, the dress she had on had been fine. But now the fabric smelled musty and had even become somewhat grimy. "You deserve an upgrade," he murmured. "And this one—this one is worthy of you."

He slipped the old dress from her shoulders, folding it carefully, almost reverently, though his nose wrinkled at its faint odor. "I suppose I'll have to burn this one." He sighed. "It served its purpose."

Lifting the new gown, he slid it over her frame, his hands lingering as though afraid to tear the delicate seams or dislodge a single pearl. "Seed pearls. Satin. A touch of lace," he murmured, his voice filled with pride. "You'll outshine every bride that's ever walked down an aisle."

He eased her upright, noting again how small she had grown, then laid her back against the pillows. He smoothed the satin across her hips, then stood back to admire his work. "Perfect," he breathed. "Perfect."

For a moment he only looked at her, his chest rising and falling with emotion. Then, with the air of a man enacting a sacred ritual, he lifted the old veil from her face. Slowly, carefully. Just as he would have done on their wedding day.

He bent close, brushing his lips across hers. Her mouth was stiff, unyielding, but he kissed her as though she had responded. His fingertips lingered on her cheek, then trailed lightly down the bodice of the gown.

Abruptly, he stopped. Something jarred him. He frowned. "No. That color's all wrong."

The bright red lipstick smeared across her lips clashed harshly with the pale beauty of the dress. "Garish. Cheap," he muttered. He fetched a tissue from the knapsack at his side and carefully wiped the lipstick from her mouth. Then he sorted through a small handful of tubes, selecting a delicate pink. With painstaking care, he painted her lips, putting the color on thickly—the way he liked it, the way he could taste it.

He leaned back to study her. Then smiled. "There. That's better. Even kissable."

This time, his kiss lingered. His imagination filled in the warmth, the softness, the gratitude he was sure she felt, although she couldn't quite express it. He knew she loved him, just as he did her.

He stood up straight, knowing it was time to leave. Knowing people might wonder where he'd been if he stayed away too long.

But he couldn't do it—he couldn't leave her just yet. She was too beautiful. For now, he just needed a few more short moments with her. He climbed onto the bed and lay beside her, curling one arm over her, and resting his hand atop the pearls on the bodice of her gown. He closed his eyes, exhaling as if finally at peace. "This is first gift of many, my darling," he whispered. "After all ... what bride doesn't deserve lots and lots of gifts?"

CHAPTER 3

Tuesday, 9 a.m. – 4 days, 6 hours before the wedding.

"I really did want to make it to your apartment last night, Angie," Paavo said into the phone as he sat at his desk the next morning. His desk blotter was already scattered with notes, a half-empty cup of coffee, and three separate witness statements he'd been cross-referencing. "But you know how it is after a murder. How many times have I told you the first few hours are crucial? That's when people's memories are sharpest—such as they are—and any physical traces are least likely to have been destroyed."

He paused to listen, rubbing at his temple with two fingers. "Yes, I know you know that. But it's still the only explanation I have for not showing up at your place last night. As I said, I'll see you tonight for sure—"

Not a good thing to say, he learned, as she cut him off to explain further. He turned in his chair, staring out at the homicide's bureau—one big room where the six inspectors had their desks, file cabinets, bookshelves, computers, and stacks of papers. The voices of the other inspectors drifted around him. His hand tightened on the phone and it took all his concentration to keep his voice as calm and peaceful as it needed to be, given the circumstances. "Of course, I remember you said you'll be meeting with girlfriends tonight. It's just that I forgot it's already Tuesday—"

That, he discovered was an even worse thing to say. He held the phone away from his ear until she wound down enough for him to get a word in. "Look, forgetting it's Tuesday is easy to do. It's just something between Monday and Wednesday. I won't forget when Saturday arrives. Saturday is special, okay? I'll be there. So, calm down."

Strike three...

"No, I'm not telling you ... Angie, you're really not calm. You're getting much too upset over nothing. Angie, listen ... Angie? Wait! Angie? Are you still there? Hello?"

The line went dead. Paavo sighed, tossed the phone onto the desk, and ground his teeth. Her last ridiculous words about being "the height of serenity" were still echoing in his head when he realized Yosh had been listening from the next desk over, amusement written all over his face.

"Don't worry about it, Paav," Yosh said, leaning back in his chair with a grin. "She'll be back to her old self the moment the vows are said. The reception will make it all worth it—and the honeymoon'll set you two right again. Trust me."

Paavo shot him a look. "I can't imagine Nancy ever giving you grief."

Yosh laughed. "No? Let me tell you something. Some little Japanese women might look serene and shy, all 'yes, dear' and demure smiles, but trust me, they rule with an iron hand. It's the quiet ones you really have to watch. You don't cross them—ever. When Nancy says 'jump,' you know what I say?"

Paavo almost smiled. "How high?"

"To start. But then I tack on, 'Is it all right if I come down after I jump, dear?'"

That finally drew a chuckle out of Paavo—the image of his huge, Sumo-wrestler size partner floating in the air, waiting for his wife, half his size, to determine if he dared come back to earth—not only amused him, but even eased the tension between his shoulders. Yosh had a way of doing that.

Together they headed out to continue investigating the bridal shop owner's murder, canvassing the businesses and homes nearby for anyone who saw something or who had a working Ring or similar camera that might have caught the front of the store.

The traffic cam videos were already in their possession, but they weren't much help. Commuter traffic was thick around six o'clock, and headlights smeared into one another, while license plates blurred or were cut off by cars traveling too close. All they could see was a steady stream of vehicles passing, none slowing, none distinct.

A florist across the street had a camera trained on the bridal shop's entryway, but the angle was poor; a coffee shop next door had one that had been broken for months. They asked the usual questions. Had anyone seen customers lingering too long? Anyone suspicious entering the shop that day? But so far, they were batting zero. Customers came and went. People tried on gowns. Faces ran together, and no one had been paying close enough attention to Lillian Kobayashi's last hours.

Inside the shop itself, the crime scene techs had lifted what felt like hundreds of prints. Too many. Brides, mothers, sales-clerks, deliverymen—sorting through them all to find one belonging to a killer was going to be like looking for a needle in a haystack.

Paavo's jaw tightened. Every wasted lead, every minute slipping away, made him more aware that he was racing against two clocks: the one ticking on Lillian Kobayashi's case, and the one counting down to his own wedding day. The idea of stepping aside and leaving Yosh to carry the case, or worse—handing it to another inspector—was intolerable. Giving up simply wasn't in his DNA.

And yet, he could still hear Angie's voice in his head, talking about napkin colors as though the right shade would decide the rest of their lives.

He shook his head. Unfortunately, murder didn't stop for weddings.

That evening, as Angie stepped into the Sakura Restaurant, she paused a moment to take a breath and savor the transformation from a fog-damp San Francisco street to the interior's warm, lacquered glow. Paper lanterns hung low from the ceiling, their red silk shades diffusing light into a gentle glow on the polished ebony tables. A bubbling koi fountain gurgled softly in the corner, and the faint clatter of chopsticks rose above the low hum of conversation. The scent of grilled teriyaki and sesame oil wrapped around her like an embrace, and for the first time all week, she felt her shoulders loosen. She really was looking forward to this girl's night out.

The hostess led her past a row of booths draped with bamboo screens to a low table near the window. From there, Angie could watch the street traffic—buses grinding past, couples strolling arm in arm—but the interior of Sakura was like another world. She smoothed her dress, a silky jade-green wrap she had chosen precisely because it made her feel festive without screaming *bride-to-be.*

She was surprised to feel a flutter of anticipation. It wasn't often she looked forward to a "girl's night"—her schedule had been wedding planning, fittings, endless lists—but tonight, she found herself oddly eager. Maybe it was because the gathering had been Nona Farraday's idea.

Colleague, yes. Confidante? Hardly. Angie had always thought of Nona as one of those women who kept her guard up, her emotions boxed away with the tidy precision of a file cabinet. But lately, Nona had been… different. Strangely raw. Quicker to laugh, quicker to tear up. Once, she even developed a bizarre crush on Inspector Luis Calderon. Talk about crossed wires! It didn't last long—no shock there.

So, when Nona suggested the dinner, Angie realized—with a pang—that Nona was wrestling with the sense that life was slipping by.

Nona had devoted herself to her career, but even she seemed to recognize it wasn't quite the prize she had once pretended. Being the top culinary reporter for *Haute Cuisine*, a glossy little foodie magazine with more ads than articles, wasn't exactly a golden ticket. Sure, the magazine catered to high-end appetites —pages filled with gleaming copper pots, imported cheeses, boutique wines, and glossy spreads of Michelin-starred dishes —but the staff was tiny. Three reporters, a handful of recipe testers, and photographers who moonlighted between shoots. The articles were mostly filler between the ads.

Nona had poured herself into it anyway; all while, the years ticked by. Never married. No boyfriend now. Angie had sensed that truth weighed heavily on her.

That was why Angie had been careful in her invitations. She'd asked her best friend Connie Rogers along—Connie, who had been married, then divorced, carried the sharp wit of someone who had survived disappointment and still had her humor intact. Then she'd thought of Scout. Young, ten years Nona's junior, but still single and on her own feet after a painful past. With a little help from Angie, Scout's bakery had become a bright success. Angie often popped by to give moral support along with baking tips—which were needed far less often these days.

Four of them. Just enough to fill a table without the air of a hen party.

Scout arrived first, cheeks pink from the wind and bringing the faint scent of butter and flour with her, as if the bakery clung to her skin. She wore her usual quirky style—this time a mustard cardigan dotted with enamel pins, over a skirt patterned with teacups. "Angie!" she cried, sliding into the booth. "This place smells like heaven."

"Wait until you taste the food," Angie said with a grin.

Connie bustled in just minutes later, all brisk energy and bright lipstick, hairspray daring her blonde hair to move a single lock despite the weather, and a soft blush-pink cashmere sweater setting off her pearls. She leaned across the table to hug both Angie and Scout, and then pulled out a chair and sat like a woman who had learned long ago to take care of herself. The three fell easily into chatter, trading stories and laughter, and not bothered at all by the gentle sound of shamisen strings.

It was twenty minutes later before Nona appeared, brisk as ever, her heels clicking against the floorboards. She gave a rushed apology and ordered a vodka martini as if she needed it to breathe. Angie noticed, not unkindly, how Nona's eyes darted over the table, sizing up everyone.

By the time Nona had finished her martini, the meal had arrived. Sashimi platters held delicate slices of tuna and yellowtail, their edges glistening like jewels. A tempura basket was filled with golden and crisp fried shrimp and vegetables, mingling with the tang of pickled ginger. And the main entre—a bubbling hot pot of sukiyaki. The server set it down in the center of the table, steam rising fragrantly as thinly sliced beef, tofu, and vegetables simmered in a broth of soy and sweet mirin.

Each of them was given a little porcelain cup of warmed sake, the almost clear liquid deceptive in its strength.

The conversation started light. Scout teased Connie about her new Pilates instructor. Connie teased Angie about her obsessive wedding planning. Nona, after her martini and two thimbles of sake, began to look less brittle and more animated.

But when the talk turned to Angie's upcoming wedding, her tone shifted.

"You're deserting me," Nona said suddenly, chopsticks poised in midair. "Running off into married bliss."

Angie set down her chopsticks. "Hardly deserting. I'm not going to vanish into thin air. I fully intend to keep working—something in food, of course. As soon as the 'bride stuff' is over."

Nona arched a brow. "Funny. You seem radiant enough about all the 'bride stuff.'" Her voice was edged with something Angie couldn't quite place.

Angie gave a short laugh. "Radiant, maybe. But don't confuse that with calm. I've learned that 'blushing bride' doesn't mean embarrassed. It means furious at everything that can go wrong. Although," she added with a small smile, "so far this week's been smooth. Mostly."

"Disaster averted," Scout said wryly.

Connie leaned in, grin flashing. "Her big day! We all say it. Honestly, no one believes a queen's coronation would be more trouble to pull off!"

Angie rolled her eyes, though warmth flushed her cheeks.

That was when Nona set down her sake cup with a decisive clink. "At least you didn't buy your dress at Forever After on Geary."

Angie's brow furrowed. "What do you mean? I know that place. The owner was very sweet. Helpful, too, but I couldn't find what I wanted there."

"You mean she *was* sweet," Nona said.

Angie stilled. "Was?"

"You don't know? She was murdered."

The word seemed to still the air itself. Chopsticks hovered in midair. Connie's mouth fell open. Scout gave a sharp gasp.

"Murdered?" Angie repeated.

"In her shop," Nona said, her tone oddly matter-of-fact. "Someone killed her and stole a wedding dress."

"That doesn't make sense," Angie said quickly. "Those gowns have to be altered, fitted—why steal one? Unless—unless it was someone she knew?"

"How can this be news to you?" Nona asked, frowning at her.

"Why should I know?"

"It's Paavo's case," Nona said, her gaze intent.

Angie stared at her, pulse quickening. "I knew he was busy. But… I thought it was a routine case. Suicides, overdoses, those sometimes land in homicide's lap for review. Not a bridal shop murder."

"Strange, isn't it?" Nona rubbed her chin, eying Angie.

"Paavo obviously didn't tell her so she wouldn't get upset," Connie said firmly.

Scout nodded. "Makes sense to me. He's a good guy."

Angie wasn't listening anymore. The room had grown a little too warm, the scent of soy and sesame suddenly cloying. She forced her voice to be steady. "Tell me, Nona, how do *you* know all about this case?"

"One of our photographers doubles as a crime scene photographer," Nona replied, a little too quickly. "He told me. Said it was bloody."

Angie's eyes narrowed. "Doubles as a CSU photographer?"

Nona flushed, fiddling with her cup. "Well, he's only *part-time* for us. We don't need photos every day, you know."

Scout and Connie exchanged glances. Angie took a long breath, willing herself to be calm. "Paavo will tell me when he can. He promised nothing would interfere with our wedding or our honeymoon. He'll get two weeks off, starting Saturday."

"I hope you're right," Nona sighed. She dabbed her lips with her napkin and pushed back her chair. "Well, I'd better be on my way. I have an important interview to conduct tomorrow morning. Oh, and Angie, I wanted to get together with you today because I won't be able to make the wedding on Saturday."

"You won't?"

"The magazine is sending me out of town to review a new restaurant. We're planning on expanding our territory, and this will be one of the first such reviews. It's a big one, so I really can't give up going."

"How exciting," Angie said, trying to hide her irritation that Nona wouldn't put off doing a restaurant review for a single day to attend her wedding. After all, it's a monthly magazine. Waiting a day to do a review hardly seems like it would make any difference at all. Where will you be going?"

"Mendocino."

It was only about three hours north of the city. "Super." Angie hoped she didn't sound too miffed or sarcastic.

They hugged politely at the door. Angie even managed a smile, though her irritation prickled beneath it.

When the three remaining women sat back down, Angie found she couldn't taste the last bite of sushi she put in her mouth. The restaurant's cheerful hum carried on around her, but her mind was elsewhere—circling the words like a moth drawn to flame.

A bridal shop. A murder. And a stolen wedding dress. That didn't bode well.

CHAPTER 4

ednesday, 11 a.m. – 3 days, 4 hours before the wedding

Angie fell asleep almost as soon as she got home last night from her girls' get-together. A tequila sunrise, more sake than she wanted to count, and then—because after Nona left, she and her friends were having too good a time to leave—a glass of plum liqueur over ice ended the night. She was glad she took a self-driving Waymo home, even though, when cold sober, they made her nervous. Her overactive imagination always put her in the middle of a Stephen King novel with a demonic Waymo sealing her inside with child-locks, and then sped her to places unknown while its mechanical voice crooned *"Arriving at your destination."*

Still, she'd slept well… until about three in the morning. Then her brain kicked on like a blender with the lid off, and she couldn't stop wild thoughts swirling all around her about the murder of the owner of the bridal dress shop. She got out of bed and found the card the lovely woman had given her many weeks ago—Lillian Kobayashi. She remembered the name as soon as she saw it, as well as the woman's face, and how helpful she had been even after Angie had made clear she wouldn't be buying a gown there.

By morning, Angie knew she couldn't let the day go by without doing something. She ordered a small bouquet—soft blush roses, baby's breath tucked around the edges—and drove over to the Forever After Bridal Boutique. The shop was shuttered, a CLOSED sign hanging ominously on the door's glass. Outside, flowers had already begun to gather—bouquets, sprays, even a couple of stuffed bears set beneath a makeshift memorial board. In bright pink chalk, someone had written in looping cursive: *Rest in Peace, Lillian—dear friend and neighbor.*

Angie crouched to place her flowers, adjusting them so they didn't tip against the doorframe. She was just about to step back when a voice, low and inquisitive, came from behind her.

"Were you one of Lillian's brides?"

Angie straightened quickly and turned. The speaker was a heavy-set woman in her sixties, round-cheeked, her tiny blue eyes squinting as if measuring Angie. She wore a green florist's apron smudged with pollen, and the faint smell of garden soil clung to her.

"I wasn't," Angie said, brushing her skirt smooth. "I did stop in once. She didn't have what I needed, but she gave me some great recommendations. She really wanted to help."

The woman's mouth softened into a wistful smile. "That was Lillian. Such a pity."

"Terrible," Angie agreed. "Were you a customer?"

"My goodness, no. Thirty-five years with the same man." The woman gave a tiny chuckle and patted her apron. "I run the flower shop next door. Lillian often sent her brides to me to help with the flowers for the wedding and the reception. Believe me, she was so helpful. I'm really going to miss her."

Angie hesitated, then asked, "Do you know what happened?"

The florist's eyes darted toward the shop windows, then back. "Word is she opened the door after hours. Probably knew whoever it was. If you ask me, the person had been in the shop before because it's natural when you walk inside, that you walk by the front counter. That's where Lillian placed the security camera. But they're saying the person never walked near the counter. Strange, don't you think?"

Angie frowned. "But the front counter would be where she kept her cash. Does that mean it wasn't a robbery?"

"Not exactly. They say a dress is missing. Not just any dress, mind you. One of her best."

Angie nodded. "I did hear a rumor about that."

The florist lowered her voice as if confiding a scandal. "It's not just a rumor. A dress in the window is gone. A Kennedy Blue. Worth a couple thousand."

"I think I know the one," Angie said, her hands sketching the memory in the air. "Layers of tulle, crystal-embroidered lace, ivory-champagne color. Beautiful."

The florist gaped at her a moment, as if not believing the detail Angie remembered. "Uh... yeah, I guess."

Angie's brows knitted. "But why? Who would steal a wedding gown? No bride would wear something like that, knowing the shop owner was killed to get it. I mean, I think anyone with even a smidgen of feeling would be uncomfortable in such a dress. My God, it's so morbid—like starting a marriage with a curse hanging over your head." She couldn't stop a shudder. "I find the whole thing creepy!"

"I agree completely!" the florist all but shouted her distress. "Whoever did this deserves the electric chair ... if we still used such a thing in California. Not that California would ever—" She cut herself short, shaking her head. "Still, it makes you sick."

By now, others had gathered—a couple with shopping bags, a man with a dog, a young woman clutching a latte. All lingered, ears pricked for scraps of gossip. Angie noticed one man in particular, standing apart. He was kind of skinny, wearing a sweatshirt despite the warming day, his gaze fixed—too fixed—

on the florist. His jaw worked like he was chewing over words he had no intention of saying aloud. A ripple of unease slid down Angie's spine.

She turned, meaning to mention it to the woman before her, but movement in the street caught her eye. A familiar car pulled up—Yosh at the wheel. Paavo was halfway out before it even stopped, his expression thunderous. Yosh rolled forward, clearly hunting for any spot to park, legal or not.

Paavo's eyes found her immediately. They always did. And he did not look pleased.

"What are you doing here?" His voice was low, clipped, but the weight of his disapproval landed like a rock in her stomach.

Angie lifted her chin. Instead of answering him, she turned to the florist. "This is my fiancé. Inspector Paavo Smith. Homicide. This is his case. Did he tell me about it? Did he bother to tell me who had died? No. I had to find out on my own that a woman I knew and liked had been so brutally attacked and killed."

Paavo's jaw clenched. "Hello, Mrs. Lear," he said politely to the florist. "Please excuse us." Then he took Angie's arm and guided her a few steps away.

"I didn't want to upset you," he said under his breath. "You've got enough on your mind with the wedding days away. The last thing I wanted was for you to think of this as an omen. Plus, I had no idea you knew Lillian Kobayashi."

Angie's irritation softened when she met his eyes. They were steady, serious, but she knew the way she'd been acting lately—it didn't surprise her that he'd try to shield her. She sighed. "Well, considering I've been in nearly every bridal shop in San Francisco, of course I knew her. But I understand what you're saying." She shook her head. "But really, Paavo. An omen? How superstitious do you think I am? I'm the *most* rational … well, anyway, thank goodness everything about our wedding is going smoothly now."

"Knock on wood," Paavo muttered under his breath.

"I heard that." She tightened her lips. "Now, who's the superstitious one? Just—catch the killer. Quickly. I don't want anything stealing your attention from me."

"You have my attention," Paavo said firmly. But then his gaze flicked past her, scanning the street. "Yosh is parking now. We need to recheck the crime scene."

Angie nodded. "I'll go. I don't want to slow down this investigation."

She gave the florist a wave, nodded to Yosh as he joined Paavo, and walked briskly toward her car, parked three blocks away.

Still, halfway there, she glanced back. The crowd had thinned. The flowers glowed faintly against the gray of the boutique. But the odd man was still there, standing perfectly still, his eyes hidden by shadow. For no reason she could name, Angie felt a chill, like a sudden draft against her neck. Her mother used to say it felt like someone was walking over your grave.

And, at the moment, Angie had to agree with her.

CHAPTER 5

Wednesday, 9 p.m. – 2 days, 18 hours before the wedding

Wednesday nights were usually quiet in Homicide. So even though San Francisco Inspector Rebecca Mayfield and her partner, Inspector Bill Sutter, were the on-call detectives that week, she had allowed herself the luxury of going home early.

Now she sat in her modest two-room apartment in flannel pajamas, a bowl of popcorn balanced on her lap, her ten-pound Chinese Crested Hairless/Chihuahua mix snuggled at her side. On the TV, an old black-and-white romance flickered, the kind where the lovers always met on a rainy street corner. Tears slid down her cheeks just as her cell phone buzzed against the coffee table.

The dispatcher's voice gave her an address.

With a sigh, Rebecca dried her eyes, clicked off the television, and padded into the bedroom to change. The last thing she wanted tonight was another dead body. But dead bodies didn't wait for convenient timing, and it was her job to meet them.

Thirty minutes later, she was guiding her car up the narrow, twisting switchbacks of Telegraph Hill. Police cruisers with flashing lights marked the crime scene, painting the ivy-covered walls in urgent red and blue. She pulled to the curb and was surprised by the building itself: a two-story mansion, its grandeur faded but still evident in the curved façade and wrought-iron balconies. A discreet stone plaque by the door read *La Belle Maison.*

Rebecca presented her credentials to the uniformed officer at the door. As she did, another officer stepped forward.

"Inspector Mayfield?" he asked.

At her nod, he introduced himself as Officer Carl Beamer. "My partner and I were first on scene. Multiple 9-1-1 calls came in from a party going on inside."

Rebecca followed him into the foyer. Marble tile gleamed beneath a chandelier of crystal drops. The wide staircase curved dramatically upward to the left. "The victim's up there," Beamer said, pointing. "We stopped everyone from leaving and moved them into the living room, or whatever it is, to clear the crime scene. They want to go home and are getting pretty upset."

Rebecca glanced toward the room. A marble fireplace dominated one wall, its mantel crowded with wilting flower arrangements. Sofas and armchairs were occupied by clusters of well-dressed guests—women in cocktail dresses and glittering jewelry, men in suits with ties askew. Instead of sorrow, their eyes radiated fury and frustration.

"Upset isn't the word I'd use," Rebecca murmured. "Looks more like they're ready to riot."

Near the foyer, a coat-and-hat check station stood abandoned, and beyond it stretched a hallway.

"Down there are some offices," Beamer explained. "We've got the victim's family in one for privacy."

Rebecca nodded and decided to take a quick walk through the ground floor before going up to see the body. Rebecca had learned from her colleague, Paavo Smith, who had been an unofficial mentor to her when she was first promoted to Homicide, that to do so was a good operating practice. In fact, she had seen a few situations where a homicide cop—her partner, Bill "Never-Take-a-Chance" Sutter—had made a bonehead assumption about a crime, and even destroyed some potential evidence, simply because he hadn't taken a moment to look over the location beyond the exact spot where the body was found.

Not that Sutter couldn't be a good cop when he wasn't hungry, tired, wanting to get home to watch some sports game on TV, or simply afraid to get involved in a dangerous situation that might lead to his being killed in the line of duty right before his retirement—a trope on too many cop shows he'd watched over the years.

Rebecca began her circuit. Where a formal dining room once stood were now large, well-appointed men's and women's restrooms. Beyond them she found a narrow service elevator, its brushed steel doors reflecting the light like a knife blade.

Last came the kitchen: a stainless steel kingdom of gleaming appliances. Sub-Zero refrigerators loomed against one wall, while two industrial stoves, side-by-side, radiated quiet menace. Deep sinks and stainless counters stood scrubbed and ready, pots and pans hung in military precision, and enough sharp implements lined the racks to make a circus knife-thrower feel right at home. A swinging door led to an enclosed porch and, beyond that, a back alley lined with trash bins and a hulking dumpster.

"Time to head upstairs," she told Beamer, who had trailed after her obediently, notebook in hand, like a faithful intern.

Upstairs, the "ballroom" spread out like a cavern dressed for celebration. White dominated: white flowers in tall vases, white bells hanging from the rafters, white ribbon strung along the edges of the dance floor. In the center of the vast space sat only four round tables, each set for six. It looked sparse, lonely, as if someone had planned a banquet and then most of the guests never showed.

On one wall a portable bar stood abandoned, bottles and glasses waiting. Opposite, a DJ station crouched silent, its speakers still humming faintly.

Toward the back, Rebecca spotted a cluster of police officers. They stepped aside as she approached.

She drew in a breath—and gasped.

The victim lay sprawled atop an oblong table, face down on the wedding cake. A chef's knife protruded from her back, blood soaking the white satin full-length gown, pooling across the lace tablecloth, and dripping in fat crimson drops to the parquet floor.

Not only had no one told her this was a wedding reception. And no one had warned her the victim was the bride.

"Oh my," Rebecca whispered. She had seen death before, but something about a bride—a woman caught between her vows and eternity—gnawed at her heart. "Her name?"

"Taylor Redmun," Beamer said quietly. "Or, well, Taylor Redmun-Borden. The ceremony took place earlier tonight."

Rebecca forced herself to focus. "We must have over twenty witnesses. Did anyone step forward?"

Beamer shook his head. "It's hard to believe, but all we've heard is that no one saw anything other than the fact that the bride came through those swinging doors." He pointed to doors not far from the wedding cake. "Apparently they open to a small room where the caterer can stage the food he brings up on the elevator, keep extras of anything he might need, or whatever. The service elevator is at the back of the space. Anyway, the guests said the bride burst out of there, through the swinging doors, then ran and stumbled towards the cake with her arms out as if she wanted to grab it, but instead, she fell on top of it. That was when they saw the knife ... and the blood."

"Who saw it?"

"Everyone, apparently. The place went crazy—screaming, people rushing for the exits. The wedding planner, Sally

Lankowitz, managed to corral them. She told them to stay put until the police arrived."

"Where is she now?"

"In her office with Officer Donaldson. She's shaken up, but holding together."

"And the groom?"

"In the owner's office—the room I pointed out downstairs. He's with his with family and close friends. Name's Leland Borden."

"What about the bride's family?"

Beamer hesitated. "No one's come forward yet."

Rebecca let that sink in before she asked, "Any idea why she went into that anteroom?"

"None," Beamer admitted. "Some think she took the elevator back up after using the downstairs restroom, although there's one up here. But no one knows for sure."

Rebecca was about to ask about the victim's belongings when the Crime Scene Unit arrived. A photographer began snapping shots of the grisly tableau.

Moments later, Medical Examiner Evelyn Ramirez, meticulously groomed as always, and wearing practical albeit stunning outfits, high heels, and carrying designer handbags, strode in with her assistants, latex gloves already snapping into place. "One of these days, I'm going to beat you to a scene," she teased Rebecca. "But at least I've beaten Sutter, as usual."

Rebecca smirked. "And where's the challenge in that?"

It was their ritual—Rebecca and Ramirez arriving long before Rebecca's thinking-about-retirement partner. She wished he would turn in his retirement papers and get it over with instead of spending almost every waking hour pondering and talking about leaving the police force. Ironically, it seemed that whenever Rebecca was ready to give up completely on him, he would pull himself together and be as sharp as he was before he started worrying about retiring. This case, apparently, was not going to be one of those times.

Ramirez leaned over the bride. When the photographer gave the go-ahead, she carefully rolled the body to one side and then the other. The knife wound was clean, deep, and likely fatal on its own.

"It doesn't appear as if there'll be any surprises here," Ramirez said, straightening. "It's unlikely anything other than the chef's knife is the murder weapon. Given the size of the blade, it may have penetrated her lungs and caused some other horrific internal bleeding. With either injury, she could potentially walk a few feet before collapsing."

Rebecca studied the body. Even in death she could see that the victim had been an attractive woman, very slim, probably around 5'8", with long, thick blonde hair—probably extensions. She wore a wedding ring with a substantial diamond, and her dress had intricate beading that would cost a pretty penny. Now it was ruined beyond repair.

"How soon for an autopsy?" Rebecca asked.

"Tomorrow morning."

Rebecca nodded her thanks. Then she pushed through the swinging doors into the anteroom. The space smelled of stale champagne and salmon hors d'oeuvres. An empty table stood in the center, shelves along the wall stacked with cutlery, dessert plates, salt and pepper shakers, and sugar bowls. A rolling cart sat shoved to one side, loaded with dirty dishes.

No blood in sight. Rebecca guessed the gown had soaked most of it as the bride staggered outward.

She exhaled, squared her shoulders, and turned back toward the ballroom. The M.E. and CSI would handle the body now. Her job was to face the living—angry guests, grieving family, and a groom whose "happily ever after" had ended before it began.

CHAPTER 6

Wednesday, 10 p.m. – 2 days, 17 hours before the wedding

"Oh, no!" Angie collapsed in a dramatic heap onto the sofa in the living room of her penthouse apartment high atop San Francisco's Russian Hill. She'd been floating for weeks on the sheer bliss of seeing her wedding plans unfold like a well-choreographed Broadway show, and even boasting to friends and family about how perfectly everything was moving along. But now tragedy had finally struck.

It was karma—karma swooping down on her for her becoming too pleased; too complacent.

After returning from the Forever After Boutique, she had spent the rest of the day and into the evening packing up her apartment for her big move across town to the home she would share with Paavo. She was sweaty, dusty, and slightly horrified by the sheer amount of junk she had accumulated. She had piles for St. Vincent de Paul, piles for recycling, piles for discard, and a mountain of boxes destined for her new life. She'd even turned down Paavo's offer of a visit that evening (unheard of!), because she felt too tired and grungy.

And then, somewhere between boxing up old shoes and

tugging a pale green sweater from her closet—the sweater she had *always* hated—disaster revealed itself.

That realization, more than fatigue, had caused her collapse.

The disaster hadn't been about dust bunnies or cardboard boxes. It had come the moment she tossed that pale green sweater into the donation bag. She'd never even liked the color —green made her look seasick. Yet as the sweater fell into the bag, she was struck with a horrifying revelation.

Something about her wedding was not perfect.

And for Angie Amalfi, that was as intolerable as showing up to a black-tie gala in flip-flops.

She had spent the last few months meticulously planning every exciting, joy-filled detail of her Big Day. From the exact minute she'd sit down for hair and makeup, to the bows tied on pews, how the favors should be presented, which size candles best communicated "romance" without looking like a séance, to the precise timing of her grand departure with her new husband (*husband!* such a gorgeous word!) to their tower suite at the Fairmont Hotel where they would spend the night before leaving on their Hawaiian honeymoon.

She believed she had thought of everything. She had lists of everything she needed to do, plus what everyone else involved needed to do. She had lists of lists. At one point, she even had a color-coded spreadsheet.

Her problem was that not only did her wedding day need to be perfect, it also needed to be *different.*

She'd been to too many weddings already. Italian families specialized in them, and Angie's clan could have staffed a small nation. Add in four older sisters with their own "special" weddings, and the bar had been raised higher than a champagne tower. Angie wasn't about to have her Big Day blend into the family scrapbook. No, hers would stand out, sparkle, and leave everyone sighing, "Now *that* was a wedding."

The ceremony itself was locked down—Saints Peter and

Paul Churchin North Beach, aka "the Italian Cathedral of the West" as San Franciscans called it—same as her parents, same as her sisters. No wiggle room there. Which meant the reception had to carry the flair.

That's where the real battles had been fought. Getting La Belle Maison booked on her date was like scaling Mount Everest in heels. Most couples needed to wait at least a year. Finally, desperate, she had called her cousin, Richie Amalfi, who seemed to know his way around the city and its movers-and-shakers better than anyone else she could think of. True to form, Richie had been friends with the owner, John Lodano, from way back. About a week after talking to him, Richie was able to get La Belle Maison booked for her afternoon wedding. It had cost her father "a bit extra." Well, *quite* a bit extra. But when she walked into that reception, it would all be worth it.

Chef Maurice of Wholly Matrimony Caterers had been the next hurdle. Known for his culinary genius, his schedule was tighter than a jar of pickles. With a generous bonus, he'd agreed not only to create the French-inspired reception feast but also to cater Friday night's rehearsal dinner.

And that was where catastrophe had reared its ugly green head.

Angie had arranged for the rehearsal dinner to take place on a cruise ship, complete with sweeping bay views, a full Italian spread, and Finnish desserts, a lingonberry pie and cloudberry mousse, as a nod to Aulis Kokkonen, the man Paavo called his "step-father." Aulis had raised Paavo and his older sister after his mother had been forced not only to leave her children, but to stay away from them forever. Paavo was never told anything at all about his father, and he'd grown up with the idea his mother simply didn't want him and his sister and had abandoned them. Only as an adult did he discover the tragic circumstances that had led to Aulis taking him in and had caused Aulis to keep everything about his parents a secret.

Learning all this had made Angie treasure Paavo and Aulis even more, along with wanting everything about their wedding to be perfect...until the green sweater threw everything into chaos. It reminded her that she had ordered little thank-you boxes of perfume for her bridesmaids and cologne for the groomsmen, and that she planned to give them out during the Friday night rehearsal dinner.

But the boxes would be wrapped in lime-green paper and tied with lime-green bows rather than the white paper and ribbon as she had originally thought. That meant she didn't want the caterer to use the lemon-yellow napkins she had chosen, but preferred that he use white ones. She didn't want her table setting to look like the world's saddest fruit salad.

Her sisters were in charge of the caterer, but if she called to complain, they would tell her she was being ridiculous. Her sisters had long since staged a mutiny, refusing to answer her calls, texts, or even desperate Facebook posts. "You're bordering on harassment," Frannie had scolded before blocking her. Blocked. By her own flesh and blood. The nerve!

They didn't understand. They thought "everything going well" was good enough. But Angie Amalfi had never been a "well enough" woman.

Which meant she had to act.

Okay, even she had to admit that the color of gift wrap clashing with the color of table napkins was small, but she had wanted everything to be perfect. The thought of the imperfect table setting was like a toothache. Since her sisters were ignoring her, she decided to take matters into her own hands and put in a call to Wholly Matrimony. No one answered, as expected that time of night.

She left a message, her voice tight with urgency. "This is Angie Amalfi. Something very important has come up regarding Friday night's dinner. Please call me as soon as possible."

But then, before she hung up, she froze. What if her treacherous sisters had already warned Chef Maurice not to take her calls? What if he ignored her message?

Her eyes narrowed. Oh, no. She would *not* be ignored.

"Or better yet," she said into the phone, a spark of steel filling in her chest, "I'll be there in the morning."

CHAPTER 7

Wednesday, 11 p.m. - 2 days, 16 hours before the wedding

Rebecca and Bill Sutter, who had finally shown up at the crime scene, were seated in the events coordinator's office. It was a pretty room done in pastel blues and yellows giving it a French country flair. They sat at the small round table where Sally Lankowitz usually met with clients. Clearly, the office had been decorated to give potential customers a relaxed, welcome feeling.

Sutter nodded at Rebecca, indicating that although he was the senior homicide inspector, she was to take the lead on this case. He was in his late fifties, with short gray hair, watery gray eyes, and from the way he was acting since walking into the events hall, didn't like having anything to do with wedding receptions. He was divorced.

"Ms. Lankowitz," Rebecca said, her hands folded as she leaned slightly towards the woman, "I understand you were the one who stopped the guests from making a mad dash out the door. Thank you for that. Now, could you please describe everything you saw and did?"

Sally shifted her red-framed glasses higher on her nose. She wore a plain but expensive black dress—the sort that would let her unobtrusively fit in with guests as she did her job. "I was looking for the bride because it was time for the cake cutting. I was surprised that she wasn't in the ballroom. I asked Leland, the groom, if he knew where she was, but he thought she was talking with one of the bridesmaids. I looked around, but I still didn't see her."

"Were all the bridesmaids in the ballroom?" Rebecca asked.

"I'm not sure. There were only three—it was a small wedding, as you saw. I'm not sure why they held it here, except that we're famous. But the bride paid for a lot more space than she needed, hiring this entire hall."

"And then what?"

"Well, I started walking around the room looking for her. Come to think of it, one of the bridesmaids may also have been missing. I know I saw two of them—their dresses are an ice blue shade—and I assumed the bride was with the third. I was heading for the stairs to check the ladies' room on the ground floor, when the door to the back of the hall swung open hard, and smacked loudly against the wall. The bride stumbled forward and kind of ran and staggered straight towards the cake. My first thought was that she had overindulged." Sally took several deep breaths before continuing. "When she fell onto the cake, I saw the knife sticking out of her back. It was horrible! Beyond horrible. For a moment, I'm sorry to say, I froze."

"What happened after you saw her?"

"Well, the swinging door banging hard against the wall caught everyone's attention. And when they saw the way Taylor was moving, several stood and watched. After she fell, it was sheer pandemonium. The group surged towards her, with people shouting to call nine-one-one. But then someone screamed that she was dead. Several people turned as if to run from the place. Somehow, I thought to shout that they had to remain here, that we had to find out what had happened."

"Did they listen?"

Sally swallowed hard. "I'm not sure what would have happened if the best man hadn't spoken up. His name is Darrel Gruber. He said everyone needed to stay to put, that they needed to be there to support and help Leland Borden, the groom. Leland, or Lee as his friends call him, had run to Taylor, and he was just standing next to her, not moving, not touching her, and looking completely shocked. At the best man's words, people quieted down—or at least stayed put." A sudden tear began to roll down her cheek, and she brushed it away.

"That's good," Rebecca murmured, reminding herself that for a person like Sally Lankowitz who normally dealt with happy occasions, coming face-to-face with murder had to be traumatic. "So tell me, how did everyone end up downstairs?"

Sally tried hard to compose herself. "One of the attendees was a retired police officer. I think he was one of the groom's uncles or something. He told everyone they needed to go down-stairs and wait for the police to arrive, and to clear the crime scene."

"So no one doubted she had been murdered?" Sutter asked, finally joining in the questioning.

"Not after seeing that knife in her back." Sally's answer was little more than a whisper, but then she faced Sutter with a question in her eyes. "Except that, how many brides are murdered on their wedding day? I tried to tell myself, and maybe others did as well, that she'd backed into the knife, or fell onto it somehow. But that's very hard to believe."

"True," Sutter said with a grimace.

Rebecca asked, "Did Taylor ever express anything to you that gave an indication she was worried or afraid of something happening at her wedding?"

"Quite the opposite." Sally pursed her lips. "She had been

given a part in a movie, and everyone knew how excited she was to get the role."

"She was an actress?" Rebecca asked.

"So she said. That was the reason for the Wednesday wedding. She needed to be on location in Mexico on Friday. That change was no problem for us. Wednesday is scarcely a busy day for weddings or any other receptions here."

"Had the wedding been booked long before today?"

"No. Not at all. Two weeks, that's all. As I said, Wednesdays are quiet here. The only problem was Taylor herself. She was the type of bride who kept changing her mind and demanding that we jump through hoops to accommodate her every whim." Sally's jaw clenched, and she tightly clasped her hands together. "So much for all her demands now."

Rebecca and Bill Sutter took over the owner's office to hold interviews with the wedding party. It was far more formal, staid, and expensively decorated than Sally Lankowitz's. It was the sort of room, the two homicide inspectors decided, more likely to cause some nervousness in a guilty person.

Leland Borden, the groom, was the first person they called in. He was about 5'9", medium build, with thinning brown hair, the sides and back had been cut impossibly short, and lots of gel made the top stand upright in a skinny front-to-back fringe. He looked as if he was in a state of shock as he approached them. Both inspectors stood.

"I'm sorry for your loss," Rebecca and Sutter murmured. They introduced themselves and gestured towards a seat. He all but fell into it. They could smell the alcohol on his breath.

"Mr. Borden," Rebecca began, "can you tell us where you were when you last saw Taylor?"

"Where? In the ballroom, of course."

"Did you talk to her?" Sutter asked.

"No. I was getting myself more champagne. Taylor doesn't like me to drink, but I really wanted to, so I went ahead. I didn't think she'd fuss at our wedding, after all. But I also didn't want to, like, shove it in her face."

"How long was that before ... before she stumbled into the room and onto the cake?" Rebecca tried to think of a better way to phrase that, but couldn't.

"I don't know. Fifteen, twenty minutes, I guess. I was talking to people."

"Who?"

"I don't know. A lot of them." He ran his fingers through his hair and then glared at the shiny goop that stuck to them. "I had my champagne, and I was being a good host, I guess.

"Did Taylor have any concerns about anyone wanting to harm her? Did she ever talk to you about anything like that?"

"Not at all." He began to choke up. "Everyone loved and admired her. The only problem could have been that some people were jealous of her. She was beautiful, successful, and was going to have a great career in movies."

"Do you think that's why your"—Sutter hesitated—"wife was murdered?"

Borden's lips tightened. "All I know is someone murdered her. People don't stab themselves in the back, do they, Inspector?"

"I haven't seen any members of her family here," Rebecca said. "Does she have any family?"

"She does." He didn't even attempt to hide the bitterness in his tone. "Her folks are in Chicago. Her father is in memory care, but her mother was going to come. Then, at the last minute, her bitch sister, Olive, talked her mother into staying home. She said it wasn't worth the time or money it would take to travel to San Francisco since Taylor didn't have time to spend with her. Taylor was a very busy person, but she was furious that her sister would have interfered that way."

"So neither her mother nor her sister, Olive, attended?" Rebecca asked.

"Correct."

"What do you think happened to Taylor?" Sutter abruptly asked. "Who wanted her dead?"

Borden clenched his fists. "I don't know. I just don't know."

After Leland Borden left, Rebecca and Sutter talked to his parents and his brother, Mason. Each of them seemed completely baffled by everything that was going on. The only thing Rebecca picked up was that they didn't know Taylor well at all. The parents had only met her once before, even though they only lived thirty miles from the city, and the brother, who had come up to San Francisco from Los Angeles for the wedding, had only met her the day of the wedding. The parents had invited her to dinner many times, but she was always too busy to accept. Leland's mother seemed resentful of that, but it was hardly a killing matter.

Finally, the family was allowed to leave, and then Rebecca and Sutter quickly questioned the other guests, each taking half, saving the members of the wedding party last.

It was getting close to two o'clock in the morning before they got to the bridesmaids and groomsmen. Between shock and booze, no one was thinking or speaking clearly. They had brought bottles of bourbon and scotch, plus a bag of ice, from the wet bar down to the living room, and proceeded to empty the liquor. They were soon sent home.

The kitchen staff was saved for last. The murder weapon had been a part of the knife set from the kitchen and had been used to carve the roast beef that was served. No one could remember if it was returned to the kitchen after dinner with what remained of the roast beef, or if it had been left in the anteroom with other used cutlery.

Finally, the kitchen staff was also let go.

Alone in the office, Rebecca and Sutter faced each other. They were also tired and sat on each end of the leather sofa that graced the room. "What do you think?" Sutter asked, stifling a yawn.

"Other than the groom, I didn't see one honest tear over Taylor's death." Rebecca put her elbow on the sofa's arm and rested her head in her hand.

"I noticed. Very strange, considering they're supposed to be her close friends."

"But they weren't. They were people she would be working with on a movie."

"Yeah, some movie." Sutter smirked. "*Outbreak.* It sounds like a movie about acne, not people from outer space who eat steel, and as a result, destroy our skyscrapers, bridges, and appliances. Why doesn't anybody make good movies anymore like *Doctor Zhivago?*"

Rebecca did a double-take. Did Sutter actually have a heart?

"Those bridesmaids were odd," Rebecca said, sitting straight again and trying to clear her head. "Not close to her at all."

"No one was," Sutter said, rubbing his eyes. "Except the groom."

One of the questions they always asked each individual when dealing with a group, was who they were with at the moment of the "incident."

"Did you find anyone who was alone or talking to no one?" Rebecca asked.

"Nope," Sutter said. "Everyone said he or she was talking with someone else. As far as I can tell, although I'll go over my notes again later, all the so-called clusters of conversations seemed to back each other up. But both the groom's buddies and the movie people were really packing away the booze and probably started doing so long before the murder. So they could have been talking to the wall, for all some of them knew—the groom included."

"Agreed. But if they're right in what they told you, we've got a murder that took place in a room where the bride was supposedly alone—although why she would go into that room was anybody's guess—she was stabbed, no one cared but the groom, and all of them had alibis. Does that sum it up so far?"

Sutter nodded. "It does."

Rebecca frowned. "That's what I was afraid of."

The two walked down the hall to see John Lodano, the owner. He was the only person not connected with police work who remained. A balding man, with a large head and hang-dog expression, he sat in the reception area, seated on a sofa and drinking coffee to stay awake. He had left the wedding after the dinner was served to go home and nap while cake, toasts, and dancing were going on. He had planned to return after the party ended to oversee the clean-up, but Sally Lankowitz's startling phone call had changed those plans.

"You can go home, now, Mr. Lodano," Rebecca said. "We'll contact you if we need any more information. The Crime Scene Unit will be here for a few more hours tonight. You've met the lead detective, Inspector Hwang. He'll make sure everything is locked up when they leave. This building is now a sealed crime scene, and everyone will need to stay out of it. We'll let you know as soon as we can release it back to you."

"You've got to be kidding." Lodano's body seemed to swell up as he spoke. "What do you mean stay out? How long? I have wedding receptions coming up. Big ones, on both Saturday and Sunday."

"We'll release it as soon as possible, but it all depends on how the investigation goes. If we quickly find the killer, we'll open it immediately. If not, we may need to hold on to it until we know we've checked everything. This is such a large facility, with so many nooks and crannies, that it might take a while."

"How long," Lodano asked, his voice low and deadly, "is a while?"

"We understand the importance of reopening your business." Rebecca tried to calm him. "I promise we'll be as prompt as possible, but we must be thorough. Usually we keep the crime scene no more than three or four days. We'll try to have it back to you by Sunday or Monday. Probably no later than Tuesday."

"How can I disappoint my customers who have been planning their wedding receptions here for months and months?" he bellowed. "I need to have my hall back."

"I'm sorry, but a woman was murdered here tonight." Rebecca's words were firm, her gaze every bit as lethal as his had been to her. "Catching her killer takes precedence over a party. Don't you agree?"

He shut his mouth and walked ahead of her out the door.

CHAPTER 8

***T**hursday, 9 a.m. - 2 days, 6 hours before the wedding*

Angie practically bounced out of bed that morning filled with cheer, determination, and the kind of reckless optimism only a bride two days from matrimony—and one crisis away from meltdown—could muster.

The sun was shining, the birds were chirping, and in Angie's mind, the entire universe was on the road to delivering her perfect wedding day.

Yes, she still had the lemon/lime napkin "disaster" simmering in the background, but in her world that was no more than a fly in the soup. Annoying, yes. But with the right spatula, a dash of willpower, and maybe a little garnish, she could fix it. Besides, her errand to Wholly Matrimony gave her the perfect excuse to check on the pièce de résistance: the wedding feast itself.

After all, Angie Amalfi wasn't just *a* bride. She was a Cordon Bleu alum, a gourmet cook, and the only Amalfi daughter foolish enough to promise three hundred relatives they'd leave her wedding reception sighing happily instead of heading straight to MacDonald's for burgers since they were still hungry. Failure was not an option.

Her menu was, in her opinion, genius: a prelude of French cheeses, goose liver pâté, and bread so crusty it could double as a weapon. Then escargot—snails dressed with enough butter and garlic to make you forget you were eating ... *snails*—followed by onion soup drowning in Gruyère, scallops shimmering in even more butter, a salad with a buttermilk–crème fraîche dressing, and a main course of veal in cream sauce with wild rice capable of reducing grown men to tears. Dessert was a small apricot clafoutis crowned with whipped cream and almonds, a finale so elegant it practically demanded a standing ovation, but small enough not to interfere with the even more delicious wedding cake: a towering rum-soaked Italian cream masterpiece, equal parts architecture and alcohol delivery system. It was less a menu than a five-act opera. And Angie was both composer and conductor.

Nothing, absolutely nothing, could spoil her mood.

Until the phone rang.

She was halfway out the door when her cell phone buzzed, sharp and shrill. She was tempted to ignore it. Nothing was more important than Wholly Matrimony.

But a glance at Caller ID stopped her cold. The call was from John Lodano, the owner of La Belle Maison.

Her pulse skipped like a scratched 78 rpm record when she saw his name. Surely, he was calling to assure her everything was working out just as planned—to tell her she needn't worry about a thing. Or, maybe he just wanted to say how honored he was to host her Big Day.

She answered the call.

Within thirty seconds, her cheerful morning had curdled like milk left in the sun. Lodano wanted to come over "for a discussion."

"What discussion?" Angie had demanded.

"It'll take ten minutes," he said. "I'll be right over."

Ten minutes later, she opened her door to find a man who looked as if he'd been boiled for stock. The suave, puffed-up business owner she remembered was gone. This Lodano was pale, sweaty, tugging at his tie as though it were a noose.

She invited him in, her stomach fluttering with nervous tension.

And then—sounding like a crème brûlée carmelized topping cracking under a spoon—he announced: "The reception hall has been declared a crime scene."

Angie stared. Blinked. Tried to swallow, but her throat had gone as dry as trying to eat biscotti without coffee. She guessed he had broken the news as gently as possible, all things considered. But how gently could one explain to a bride that her long-awaited wedding reception location was in peril? Especially when he was forced to include that, unless the police released it, she was going to have to find another location for her reception.

She couldn't believe what had just happened. Her reception a crime scene? No, this was a sick joke—sort of like putting pineapple on a pizza.

"Oh, sure," she croaked. "No problem at all. I'll just whip up a new venue like a batch of scones. Maybe the Vatican's free this weekend. I'll check."

"There was … a death," Lodano added, his tie now hanging limp as overcooked fettuccini.

"A death?" Angie squeaked. "What do you mean, a death? Someone choked on an escargot? Slipped on the béchamel? What?"

"It appears to have been a murder."

"Murder?" The word came out so high-pitched, the pigeons outside scattered.

For one insane second, Angie felt a flicker of hope. "Well. Okay. That might not be *so* bad."

Lodano blinked. "Not … bad?"

"I mean—not *good*! Obviously murder is bad. Horrible! Tragic! Awful!" She flung her hands in the air, a cross between praying and desperation. "But my fiancé is a homicide inspector. If anyone can clear this scene before Saturday, it's Paavo." She knew she was blathering, but couldn't stop. "I'll just add it to his honey-do list. Buy wine, polish shoes, solve murder, release banquet hall. Believe me, if anyone can do it, Paavo can."

Lodano looked like he might faint into her sofa. "I... I wouldn't count on that. The detectives seemed... very serious."

"Which detectives?"

He fumbled for business cards. "Rebecca Mayfield and Bill Sutter."

Angie stiffened. Okay, Bill Sutter was easy. That man would vanish like a paper napkin in a tornado at the first whiff of pressure. But Rebecca Mayfield? Rebecca Mayfield, with her judgey eyes and her inconvenient by-the-book approach to her job? Disaster.

Angie crossed her arms. She had been quite sure Inspector Mayfield wanted Paavo for herself—everyone in Homicide knew Rebecca had had a crush on him. The thought of tall, blonde, beautiful—somewhat—Rebecca working alongside Paavo had irked and worried Angie when she first met him. Short, brunette Angie had spent a lifetime feeling second fiddle to tall, buxom blondes from her high school days when Jimmy Soares—who she had a major crush on—had invited five-foot-ten, DDD-cup Dinah Turner to the prom instead of her. It had broken her heart.

But this time, mercifully, Angie had won. She'd gotten her man. And she'd be damned if Rebecca Mayfield—or anyone— was going to wreck her wedding feast. She leaned forward, giving John Lodano a glare sharp enough to fillet a trout. "Somehow, some way, my reception will happen at La Belle Maison."

Lodano's Adam's apple bobbed like a meatball in sauce. "M-Maybe you should call your caterer. Just in case."

She exhaled. Much as she hated to admit it, the man wasn't wrong. If Mayfield had her icy hands on the crime scene, nothing was safe.

"I'll consider it," Angie said tightly.

Lodano leapt to his feet, like a waiter fleeing a flaming baked Alaska. "You might try outside the city. And, uh—please—if you see your cousin Richie, tell him this wasn't my fault. *It wasn't my fault!*"

"I'll pass it along," Angie said flatly as she also stood. Then, unable to resist, she asked, "So … who died?"

He hesitated. "I doubt the name will mean anything to you."

"Try me."

"A young woman. Taylor Redmun."

Angie gasped. "Somebody killed Bridezilla?"

Lodano winced. "I'm afraid so." Then, realizing what he'd just admitted to, his lips quivered like a collapsing soufflé.

They parted awkwardly. Angie shut the door with a decisive click and leaned against it, her mind whirling. Bridezilla was dead. Her reception hall was a crime scene. And Rebecca Mayfield was circling like a shark in Nordstrom Rack heels.

But Angie already had one prime suspect in mind: Sally Lankowski.

Again alone, Angie sank into the petit point sofa, her hands folded in her lap like a schoolgirl waiting for scolding. Her feet were flat on the carpet, but she felt anything but grounded. The world tilted as she stared blankly at the far wall, her mind replaying John Lodano's every word.

She was in shock. Complete, unadulterated shock.

She hadn't liked Bridezilla—who could?—but the thought of any bride, on her wedding day, ending up dead was horrific. Tragic. A shiver ran through her. Add to that the murder happening at La Belle Maison—the very temple of food and elegance was horrifying.

But as much as her heart went out to the victim, reality barged in like an unwelcome guest at a buffet. What about her own reception? With just two days left, her venue's only decoration was yellow crime scene tape.

Three hundred people. Family. Friends. Out-of-towners who had already booked flights, hotels, and who had probably been dieting all month to make room for her menu. She had promised them a feast. She had promised them an experience. She had promised them a day so memorable that their taste buds would sing opera every time they thought back on it. She had staked her reputation as being someone who could throw a truly wonderful reception—and now that reputation was going to be as non-existent as her venue.

Her blood pressure had to be at least double what it was yesterday. Maybe triple. She imagined a cuff strapped to her arm exploding like an overfilled éclair.

She couldn't help but laugh at herself over the way she'd carried on about napkin colors. What good were napkins if there was no table to put them on? No bread basket. No wine glasses clinking. No apricot clafoutis carried in triumph like a torch in the Olympic Games of Dessert.

She had two choices: collapse in tears, or do something.

And Angie Amalfi had never been one to collapse.

She grabbed her handbag, marched out the door, and went straight to the Hall of Justice. It wasn't a phone call kind of problem. Or even a text problem. This was a march-straight-into-the-lion's-den kind of problem. And maybe—if it came to it—a cry-on-the-detective's-desk problem.

She'd always found the Hall of Justice as grim as its name. A hulking gray building huddled by the freeway ramps just south of downtown San Francisco, it housed courtrooms, holding cells, and the Bureau of Inspections. But now, Angie pushed through its doors like a woman on a mission and headed straight to the fourth floor.

Angie knew the secretary, Elizabeth, and gave her a quick wave before storming inside. As always, the Homicide bureau was as messy as a kitchen after a Thanksgiving dinner: papers everywhere, files stacked like uneven layer cakes, computer monitors glowing, and along the edge, desolate interrogation rooms lurked.

Paavo was at his desk. Her Paavo. Looking calm, controlled, and devastatingly handsome. His partner and best man, Yosh, was also there, as was Luis Calderon. The other three inspectors, Mayfield, Sutter, and Calderon's partner, Bo Benson, were out—hopefully trying to determine who killed Bridezilla so she could get her wedding reception venue back.

Paavo stood when he saw her. Those blue eyes—pale and striking—met hers with concern. Angie's heart gave a treacherous flutter, but she tamped it down.

This was war. Against fate, bad luck, and Inspector Rebecca Mayfield.

"Angie! What a surprise. Is something wrong?"

"You've heard, right?" she asked, sinking into the guest chair by his desk.

His eyebrows knitted. "Heard what?"

"Where's Rebecca Mayfield?" Angie asked instead.

Paavo sat too, pulling his chair closer, his voice careful. "I suspect she's out on the case she and Bill Sutter caught last night. They're the on-call team this week."

"So they haven't solved it yet?" Angie pressed.

He frowned. "I guess not. Why are you asking?"

"What are they doing now?" she asked.

"What's going on, Angie?"

"Please, Paavo."

He grew more confused with each non-answer she gave. Finally, he stopped asking. His face stern, he said, "I haven't heard anything from them. They were apparently up most of the night and haven't come in yet this morning. Tell me why you want to know. Is someone you know involved?"

Angie drew in her breath and shut her eyes a moment, wondering how to break the terrible news to him.

She couldn't get it out. Not yet. She grabbed his hand in both of hers and squeezed, but her throat refused to form the words.

"Angie," he said softly, worry etching his face, "tell me what's happened."

Her breath shuddered. "The victim…" She swallowed hard. "She was Bridezilla."

Paavo's face tightened. "What?"

Then, the dam burst. Angie's words tumbled out like spilled sugar. "Bridezilla! The impossible bride I told you about—the one who hijacked my consultation with Sally Lankowski! She's the one who was murdered. At … at La Belle Maison!" Her eyes filled with tears, her voice broke, and shaking, she gave him the terrible news. "Our reception hall is the crime scene, Paavo."

He gawked at her. "No."

"Yes! La Belle Maison. The place I worked like a dog to get for our reception; the place I finally had to ask Cousin Richie for help in finding a space for us on their calendar. It's now the crime scene, and if the murder isn't solved by Saturday at four p.m., no, actually they'll need time to set things up—if it isn't solved by Saturday at noon, one o'clock at the latest, we won't have a place for our reception. We have three hundred people coming to see us get married, and we have no place to feed them."

As the full impact of what she was saying hit, as he thought of the untold hours she had spent obsessing over her Big Day, Paavo placed a comforting hand on her shoulder. "Angie, don't let this upset you. It has nothing to do with our wedding. We'll figure out something. If there's some strange superstition attached to—"

"A superstition?" His words made no sense. How silly did he think she was? The more she thought about it, the more annoyed she became. She pushed his hand off her shoulder, her cheeks flaming. "You think some superstition is what's troubling me? What? Something old, new, dead and blue? Is that it? Or maybe it's the one that says don't hang around dead brides before your wedding."

He sighed. "Take a deep breath." She knew he wanted to sound soothing, but as he continued, each word had the exact opposite effect. "I can imagine that having met a bride and to now learn that she's dead is a trifle, well, more than a trifle upsetting—"

"No, you take a deep breath! Do you realize what this means?" Her voice cracked. "If this case isn't solved by Saturday, three hundred guests—our family, our friends—will have no reception. No dinner. No wine. No cake! Do you know what it means to promise an Italian family food and then fail to deliver? There are vendettas that started over less!"

Paavo's expression shifted as the full weight of her words hit him. How much pride she'd invested in making this a special day, not only for the two of them, but for all her family and friends. She'd once told him that she wanted it to be a symbol of not only the love the two of them had for each other, but of the love she had for the family and friends she wanted to share this special moment with.

"I'm so sorry, Angie."

"Paavo, you've got to fix this! Find the killer. Open up the crime scene as soon as possible. Get CSI to finish up. I mean, how long does it take to dust a few fingerprints? How long does it take to bag some evidence?"

He rubbed his temples. "Angie, I don't know what I can do."

A nasty thought struck Angie, and as much as she knew she shouldn't have said it, the words were out of her mouth before she could stop them. "Does Mayfield know it's our *wedding* reception hall?"

"I don't know," he admitted. "But I know what you're thinking, and Rebecca's not like that."

"Are you sure?" Angie folded her arms. "I've heard from more than one person that she never wanted me to marry you. That we're too 'incompatible'—as if the only one who could understand you is her!"

"Angie, just stop. From what I hear, your Cousin Richie is the only guy currently hanging around her, and despite her comments to the contrary, she seems to enjoy it whenever he makes an appearance." He shook his head at the thought of Rebecca and Richie getting together. They'd kill each other before their first date ended.

She dropped her gaze. "Okay, I'm sorry. It's just that I'm so upset..."

"I know." He placed his hand on her chin. "Let me be completely honest with you. I'll talk to Rebecca and Sutter as soon as I can, *but* ... unless the case is simple and straightforward, releasing a crime scene in under forty-eight hours is almost impossible. So I suggest you start looking for a backup."

Angie's mouth dropped open. "A backup? What am I supposed to do?" Tears threatened again, but she blinked them back. "I wanted this to be perfect. For you. For everyone. I promised them perfection."

He stood and pulled her gently up with him, his touch warm and steady as he then walked her to the elevator. "We'll work it out. I'll find out where things stand on the investigation. Go home, call your sisters, start making phone calls. Don't give up yet."

She let out a shaky laugh. "Maybe we'll get lucky. Maybe some couple will have a big fight and canceled their wedding."

As the elevator bonged telling of its imminent arrival, he gave her a quick kiss, holding her close. "We'll work it out."

The elevator doors slid open, and Angie stepped inside. She forced a smile through her tears. "That's all I needed to hear."

"But," he called as the doors closed, "just in case—get a backup plan."

CHAPTER 9

Thursday, Noon – 2 days, 3 hours before the wedding
As soon as Angie left, Paavo grabbed the phone and called Rebecca.

She answered on the second ring, her voice crisp, edged with distraction. "I'm at the victim's apartment, looking for anything that might tell me who wanted Taylor Redmun-Borden dead."

"I'd like to come over," Paavo said.

A pause. Then a sharp exhale, almost a laugh without humor. "Why am I not surprised? I got a wedding invitation, remember? I know exactly where your reception was supposed to be held. We need to talk. I'll text you the address."

And she hung up.

Taylor's apartment was a disappointment before he even stepped inside. The building, crouched near the waterfront off Broadway, had once promised charm. Instead, it smelled faintly of mildew, salt air, and garbage, with the rustle of wharf rats in the shadows. The kind with tails long enough to double as jump ropes. It wasn't the kind of address Paavo expected for a bride whose nuptials had taken place at the high-priced, elegant La Belle Maison.

Inside was worse. A small, tired space, crammed with worn furniture and the stale air of a life that didn't quite match its glossy exterior. It felt wrong, off—like a stage set stripped of its props. Clearly, the groom was the one with money.

Rebecca was waiting for him in the living room, arms folded, posture tight. "So, Angie called in the cavalry. Richie warned me this morning her wedding reception's at risk, and now I'm suddenly the roadblock standing between her and happily-ever-after. You know crime scenes don't work that way."

Paavo was stunned. "Richie knew about this before I did?"

Rebecca shrugged, irritation flickering in her eyes. "He said the owner of La Belle Maison's a friend of his. Doesn't matter."

"It matters to Angie," Paavo said quietly. "She had her heart set on that reception—" He stopped himself. He'd seen Rebecca's expression sour, irritation sharpening the more he spoke. He'd just lived this scene with Angie, and now he was about to repeat it. Why was it always easier talking to his partner, Yosh? "Look. I'm only here to see if there's anything I can do to help. Anything to speed this up."

"No," Rebecca said flatly, and turned away, disappearing into the bedroom where she began riffling through the victim's closet.

Paavo followed, then asked, "Where's Sutter?"

"Talking again to the groom's parents."

"Learned anything useful yet?"

Rebecca shut the closet door with a snap. "Not much. Taylor's bridesmaids were practically strangers. None close. Her family didn't even show. Only the groom seemed to know and care about her."

Paavo frowned, thinking of Angie's family, flying in from every corner of the country, bringing casseroles, loud voices, and a tangle of love and arguments. Dysfunctional, yes. But at least they showed up.

"Her sister's in Berkeley," Rebecca added. "We told her early this morning. She was … sad. For her parents' sake. Not for Taylor's. Her parents live in Chicago, Taylor's hometown, but they haven't seen each other in years."

"Did the sister say why?"

"Nothing specific. She said, and I quote, 'Taylor was a selfish bitch and always has been.'"

That hit Paavo harder than he let on. He thought of his own family—what little remained of it—and the bleak, bitter stories he'd heard again and again on the job. The Amalfi clan, with all their chaos, suddenly seemed like a miracle.

"Any ideas yet who might've killed her?"

Rebecca shook her head, then shut the closet door. She had found nothing in there. She walked over to a nightstand, but before opening the drawer faced Paavo. "Not yet. But it was actually a strange wedding. Each of her bridesmaids was surprised to have been asked to take part. None were close friends with Taylor. In fact, I couldn't find anyone who was— other than the groom.

"Anyway, no one saw any strangers enter or leave the build- ing, and it was a small group so someone not belonging should have been noticed. But I've requested the venue's security cameras as well as any other in the immediate area to double check that. At the moment, Sutter and I have two theories. Either Taylor went to meet someone in the anteroom—a sort of pantry that leads to the service elevator downstairs to the kitchen—and that person killed her; or she decided to use the elevator instead of the stairs to go down to the women's room, and someone waited in the anteroom for her to return and killed her. My gut tells me the last is less likely. Too much left to chance."

"Who would she be meeting in secret at her wedding?" Paavo asked.

"I have no idea. Yet."

"What about motive?" he asked. "Any sense of why someone would kill her—on her wedding day, no less? Jealousy? A rival for the groom?"

"That movie crew is consumed with jealousy over all kinds of things, but I didn't sense marriage to Leland Borden was one of them."

He nodded. "Looking at the wedding party and the guests, does anyone stand out?"

"Boy, talk about the third degree, Paavo! Okay, listen, the main thing standing out with that whole weird wedding scene was that everyone was a family member or a friend of the groom, or a business associate of the bride. The business associates—her agent and people involved in a movie Taylor was going to be in—seemed to hardly know her. After a murder, people usually talk about what a saint the deceased was. In this case, they talked about how they wished they hadn't come to the wedding, except that it was on a Wednesday night and they didn't really have an excuse not to. Apparently, in 'show biz,' as one of them said, you never know when someone's career will take off, so it's best not to burn bridges."

"Sounds like a caring bunch," Paavo said.

"Very. But it also sounds like a bunch of people with no reason to kill her."

"Unless someone saw her as potential competition."

"Could be."

Paavo turned back to Rebecca's theories—Taylor meeting someone in secret, or ambushed on the way to the restroom. Both plausible. Both ugly. Paavo felt coiling ever tighter in his chest both the urgency and the impossibility of solving this before Saturday at noon.

They moved back into the living room as Rebecca ticked off her next steps. "I asked the members of the wedding to be at the bureau at one. Sutter and I will interview them individually. That might help us get to the bottom of this mess."

"And the crime scene unit?"

She shook her head. "They determined the murder weapon —a knife with a long, narrow, and very sharp blade—was part of a set used in the kitchen. It was sent up to the ballroom solely for the purpose of carving the roast beef. They also found that the bride's fingerprints are all over the facility, including the kitchen."

"Has anyone looked into the caterer?" Paavo asked.

"Not yet."

"If you can use some help…"

Before she answered, her phone buzzed. Her face tightened. It was Homicide's dispatcher. After talking a moment, she shook her head. "I don't believe it! Another dead body. This one was found under very mysterious circumstances—and she's wearing a wedding dress."

"*What?*" Paavo, too, could hardly believe it. "Not another bride."

"I don't know. But since Sutter and I are the on-call team this week. We'll have to go over there."

San Francisco Homicide used a system where two-person "on-call" teams handled all homicides in a given week or weekend and then concentrated on working those homicide cases until their next on-call turn came up. Only rarely did more than one actual homicide—if that—occur in any given period that the on-call team couldn't handle them.

Paavo felt his stomach sink. He knew that if Rebecca and Sutter pivoted to a new case, the Redmun-Borden murder investigation would take a temporary back seat. Even if they found that this latest call didn't involve a murder, it could chew up enough time to make it even more impossible to solve the Redmun-Borden murder before Saturday.

He quickly told her about the murder at the Forever After Bridal Boutique. "If you'd like," he said, "Yosh and I will handle this call for you. It could be connected to our case. But if there's any way the death is connected to your case—"

"Hold on." Rebecca arched an eyebrow. "You're thinking some deranged wedding-hating killer is running around?"

"Could be," Paavo said. "And if that's the situation, we'll work the cases together."

For a moment she looked at him, weighing it. Then her mouth twisted into something halfway between a smirk and a sigh. "You know I really should tell you to take a flying leap and keep your nose out of my cases," she said, hands on hips.

"But you understand that this is a rare circumstance, and I'm a truly desperate man."

She nodded and seemed unable to stop a smile from playing across her lips. "Yes. And, thanks to Richie—or maybe I should say, no thanks to Richie—I've come to understand the Amalfis a bit."

"Oh?"

"Let me clarify," she said, "it's not that I particularly like them, but I can sympathize with what you're facing."

Paavo couldn't help but cringe, even as he recognized why she felt the way she did. All he could say was, "Thank you, Rebecca."

For the first time, the hard line of her mouth softened, a reluctant smile tugging at the corner. "No thanks needed. And I want to add—if someone out there has declared war on brides, we're going to need all hands on deck."

Paavo's felt as if his blood turned to ice. For Angie's sake, they had to stop this killer—before "death do us part" became more than a vow.

CHAPTER 10

Thursday, 2 p.m. – 2 days, 1 hours before the wedding

Paavo contacted Yosh, and they met fifteen minutes later in the Western Addition. The neighborhood had always been a patchwork of contradictions—one block gentrified with trendy cafés and yoga studios, the next block rotting under years of neglect, as if the city had forgotten it existed.

The address they were headed toward belonged to the latter sector—the neglected, the abandoned, the forgotten. Even now, mid-afternoon, in the hazy wash of fog, the place felt diseased, the cracks and peeling paint on the old buildings like sores that would never heal.

A knot of tenants and gawkers crowded the sidewalk in front of the hulking concrete housing project. Their faces were pale and restless, eyes darting toward the entrance, then toward Paavo and Yosh as the detectives pushed through. The crowd stepped aside almost grudgingly, opening a corridor that felt less like respect and more like the passageway at an execution. Yosh gave nods and muttered greetings, trying to humanize the moment. Paavo's face remained hard, unyielding. He could feel the suspicion in their eyes, could hear the unspoken thought in the murmuring silence: *Whatever's inside, it isn't ours anymore. It belongs to death.*

Inside, a uniformed officer led them to Benny Simms, the project's building manager.

Simms looked like a man who'd been drained of blood and nourishment. His chalky skin gleamed with sweat, his stringy blond hair plastered to his forehead. His jeans were soiled, his flannel shirt streaked with stains that looked older than the tenants themselves. His hands trembled when he reached up to smooth his hair, but never quite touched it, as if even his gestures were half-hearted.

He led them down a narrow stairwell into the basement.

Each step down felt like a step deeper into a tomb. Yosh was in the lead and glanced back at Paavo, his eyes questioning. The overhead bulbs flickered and buzzed, casting the cracked concrete in a half-light. The air grew thicker, hotter, more oppressive the further they descended—saturated with the nasal-clogging dust of old cement and the metallic tang of rust. From somewhere near the boiler, steam hissed like a snake.

By the time they reached the storeroom, the air felt so hot it was almost alive, pressing against their eyes and throats.

The door was unlocked, its hinges groaning faintly as Simms pushed it wider.

As Paavo stepped through the threshold, his stomach tightened.

The woman lay on her back on a filthy mattress, her body stretched out as though posed for some grotesque portrait. The bridal gown she wore was clean—too clean—its tulle and pearls glowing faintly in the dim light. Her veil was thin, but it cascaded over her face like a funeral shroud.

But they could faintly see her features through it. Paavo put on gloves, then lifted the veil.

Her face was shriveled, mummified, the flesh pulling tight against her skull, but her lips... her lips were slicked with thick, wet pink lipstick. The color shone in the single dangling bulb's glow, obscene against the leathery ruin of her skin. The mouth was cracked and stretched, not quite into a smile—not quite—but into something that mimicked one. Almost like an imitation of joy made by someone who had never understood it.

Yosh swore under his breath. "My God." He leaned back, hand covering his mouth, but his eyes stayed locked on the corpse as though afraid it might move if he looked away. "That's not just rage. That's … devotion twisted into something monstrous."

Paavo said nothing. As soon as he saw the corpse, he realized that if the same person had killed Taylor Redmun-Borden, the perpetrator's rage against brides had lasted a long time, and his MO had completely changed. No, this wasn't the same killer. This kill was … different.

He studied the details: the mattress sagging with rot, the bridal dress without a speck of dust, the black hair still glossy beneath the veil. Whoever had done this had *cared*. Had fussed over the body, had preserved it, and had painted it.

The thought made his skin crawl.

"How did you find her?" he asked, his voice low.

Simms twitched like a marionette. "I—I never come down here. Place is creepy as hell. I only check it if a furnace conks out or something." His eyes darted to the corpse, then away. "Most of the time these rooms stay locked up tight."

"What is this room supposed to be?" Yosh asked, his tone sharp.

"Storage," Simms muttered. "But ain't nobody got nothing worth storing down here."

"Why did you look inside tonight?" Paavo pressed.

Simms rubbed his temple, then wiped his wet fingers on his jeans. "One of the tenants left me a note. Said somebody was hanging around down here. Happens sometimes—junkies, homeless, gang kids. They make it a crib. Safer than the streets, warmer than the alleys. I figured I'd better check it. Didn't figure on…" His voice trailed off. His throat bobbed as he swallowed.

"Any idea who she is?"

"Hell, no."

"Which tenant told you someone was down here?" Yosh asked.

"Hell, man, I don't know. Like I said, I got a note. People here don't talk much, especially not to rat out each other. It's a rough neighborhood."

Yosh was growing increasingly irritated. "How long have you been the building manager?"

"Uh … goin' on a year in a month or two, I guess."

"How did you get the job?"

"I heard, if I did it, I didn't have to pay no rent. I went down to City Hall. Nobody else wanted it."

Paavo wasn't surprised at that answer. He could understand no one wanting to be responsible for trying to keep tenants in a building like this happy. It would be a thankless task.

"Who else had access to this room?" Paavo asked.

"Anybody." Simms's voice cracked. "Any tenant, their friends. Anybody who wanted to jimmy the lock. Ain't hard. But it ain't my fault if somebody sneaks in, you understand? Managers before me, maybe they had keys made. I only got two. Never gave 'em out. Never."

Paavo studied him. The sheen of sweat on Simms's upper lip trembled with each shallow breath. He looked like a man caught between fear and guilt, and neither was flattering.

"When were you last in here?" Yosh asked.

"Shit, I don't know. Maybe six, seven months ago. Like I said, it's supposed to be empty. No reason for me to come in here."

"Did you ever see anyone come down here? Anyone at all?"

Simms licked his lips, his hand drifting again to his temple. "Not that I remember. But nobody comes here unless they're up to no good." His eyes flicked to the corpse again. His voice dropped. "Told you. Creepy as hell. Don't like it none."

The bulb overhead buzzed louder, then popped faintly, making Simms flinch like a gun had gone off.

Paavo nodded for Yosh to continue the questioning and began pacing the room. He ran his eyes along the walls—cracked concrete, a latticework of old pipes sweating condensation, and the heat, the oppressive heat, from the boiler. A dark, high transom window caught his attention.

"Why is that window black?" Paavo asked suddenly.

Simms turned, startled. "Oh, shit. I—I never noticed."

"Are all the basement windows painted like that?"

"Maybe. I don't know. Never paid attention." His words tumbled out too fast, as if hoping they'd bury the silence rather than fill it.

Before Paavo could press further, the sound of voices drifted down the hall, and Evelyn Ramirez swept into the room with her team of assistants. The energy shifted immediately—the corpse had already made the air oppressive, but Evelyn's arrival made it clinical, as though death were suddenly under a spotlight.

She glanced at the body and arched a brow. "Another bride?" Her tone was flat, but her eyes betrayed a flicker of unease. "Two brides and a dead bridal shop owner. Sounds like someone got a deep hatred for brides." She crouched beside the corpse, leaned close to the cracked, painted lips, and muttered, "Whoever this is, the grudge runs deep."

Simms's composure broke. He gave a strangled little cough, then bolted. His boots slapped the concrete as he vanished into the hall, not even pretending to wait for dismissal.

Nobody stopped him.

"Any chance to get fingerprints?" Paavo asked.

Evelyn crouched by the body, tilting her head like she was studying an art piece. She pinched one brittle hand delicately between her gloved fingers, as if afraid it might crumble to dust. "I'll try to rehydrate the skin," she said after a moment. "So yes, there's a chance. Just… not a comforting one." Her voice was soft, but her eyes never left the shriveled hand. "These fingers look more like dried twigs than flesh. Rehydration could work, but sometimes it only warps the skin into grotesque shapes. Sometimes the fingerprints that rise up aren't recognizable as human at all."

She straightened, pulling off her gloves with a snap. "Poor Paavo," she added almost absently, her tone slipping from clinical to personal without warning. "What a macabre collection of murders to face the week before your wedding day. The timing is … cruel."

"I know," Paavo said glumly. "And the one last night was at the place Angie had chosen for our reception. I don't know what we're going to do. It's a big hall, and now it's all a crime scene. Angie's having fits."

Evelyn's lips curled into a faint, unreadable smile. "You've got time. And things often have a way of working out for the best."

He had no idea what she meant—"for the best" wasn't part of his vocabulary. "I hope so," he muttered, then returned to the problem at hand. "As to this case—how long do you think she's been dead?"

Evelyn's expression tightened. "That's where it gets difficult," she murmured. "You know what bodies usually look like weeks and months after death. Softening. Rot. Maggots. This one…" She gestured with her chin. "No maggots. No collapse. Dried out like fruit left in the sun. Someone knew what they were doing to keep the flies away, but as for the drying—well, it's plenty warm down here, being in the basement and right next to the boiler room. With a lot of care and attention, that would do it. It's similar to what the ancient Egyptians did, something called natural mummification. I haven't had one of these before.

San Francisco is normally to humid and too cool—temperature wise—for it to happen."

"I see," he murmured.

"It'll take me a while. I'll have to see what's going on inside her, and then do some research. Whoever did this *tended* to her, Paavo. They wanted her preserved. They *cared* for her, in their own way. She isn't a corpse so much as a … a keepsake."

Yosh shifted uneasily. "How long do you *guess* she was dead?"

"Months," Evelyn said, almost whispering. "Several months… for the *body*."

"For the body?" Yosh echoed.

Evelyn nodded. "That's right. The dress looks almost new. Someone dressed her carefully, reverently. Someone wanted her to stay beautiful… even as the flesh gave way."

Paavo and Yosh exchanged a grim glance. "Could the dress have come from the Forever After shop?" Paavo asked. He checked his notes. "Tulle. Pearls. Lace."

"This one has all that," Evelyn said, hands on hips. "But so do dozens of others. The difference is…" She reached out and gently smoothed the veil further away from the face. "The lipstick. That shine is *fresh*. Hours old, not months. Someone's been with her recently. Someone touched her. Kissed her, maybe."

The silence that followed was heavy, sickening. Even Yosh's usual chatter died in his throat.

"I've got an idea," Paavo said. He stepped out of the room and phoned Angie.

"Paavo! How nice to hear from you!" she said.

"And you, but I'm calling about something that's kind of grim."

"Grim? I don't need anything else that's grim. But go ahead. What is it?"

"At the bridal shop where your friend was killed, do you

have any idea about the dress that was stolen? What it looked like, or anything else?"

"Of course. It was a lovely dress, but would have looked wrong on me. It needed someone tall and—"

"Angie, what can you tell me about it? In detail."

"Well, for one thing, it was a Kennedy Blue, and more expensive than most in the shop. And—"

"Wait, one minute." He dashed back into the storage room. "What's the label on the dress."

Evelyn signaled her assistant. "Turn her carefully. Let's check the label." Tiny buttons were undone, fabric peeled back from the stiffened body until the tag was revealed. "Kennedy Blue."

Paavo took a photograph the dress, doing his best to get nothing of the woman's face or her desiccated neck. Then he got back on the phone with Angie. "I just sent you a photo. Is this the dress you saw at the shop?"

Angie paused a moment, as if to be sure. "Yes. That's the one. Paavo, I don't like this. Where did you find it? Who's wearing it?"

"We'll talk later. Thank you."

He returned to the storeroom, his voice tight. "It's the one. The stolen dress."

The three of them stared at the figure on the filthy mattress. The veil had slipped a little lower now, half-shrouding the face in shadow, like a bride waiting for the moment she'd be revealed at the altar.

But this altar reeked of cruelty and death.

The lipstick gleamed at them from the corpse's mouth, wet, fresh, mocking.

And Paavo knew, with a hollow certainty, that somewhere nearby, the killer was smiling.

CHAPTER 11

Thursday, 3 p.m. – 2 days, 0 hours before the wedding

Angie went to the Wings of an Angel restaurant on Columbus Avenue in the North Beach area. The place was owned by three older men—ex-cons, yes, but also her friends. Over the years they'd gone from running cons to running calamari, and Angie adored them.

She sat hunched over a plate of their signature spaghetti, twirling and untwirling the noodles like she was winding yarn. Normally, she savored every bite of their sauce, a rich, savory miracle that made her sigh with bliss. The shocking secret ingredient, she'd learned long ago, was Spam. Spam in spaghetti! Somehow it worked. But today? Today the noodles could've been dental floss, and she wouldn't have noticed.

Earl White, one of the owners, slid into the chair across from her the second the last lunch customer waddled out. Earl was in his sixties and wore a thick, curly brown toupee so glossy and immovable it looked like it had been dipped in lacquer. But he still carried himself like he was a part of security at the Sands Casino in Reno. He also once worked as a bouncer in Las Vegas. But the job didn't last long, since, tough as he was, five-foot-five bouncers sometimes got bounced themselves.

"Whatza matter, Miss Angie?" he asked, his accent flattening vowels and clipping consonants like a New York deli slicer.

She sighed. "A murder was committed at the place I planned to hold my wedding reception. The whole building's now a crime scene. If Homicide doesn't release it by noon Saturday…" She slumped forward. "I'm sunk."

Earl's eyebrows shot up. "Jeez, dat's a real bum deal. I'm sorry t'hear it. Real sorry. But hey, you'll find another place, I'm sure. And you still got dat fancy French caterer, right? Maurice—what's-his-name? I shoulda known you'd get somebody big an' popular like him to cook for your weddin'. My mouth waters jus' t'inkin' about it." He smacked his lips. "I can already taste da hors d'oeuvres. Me, Butch, an' Vinnie, we never been ta a high-class shindig like you're puttin' on. T'anks for t'inkin' of us, doll."

"Of course I invited you guys. I love you!"

Earl actually blushed, which, on a man built like a fire hydrant, was strangely endearing. "We love ya too, Miss Angie."

"Thank you. But the problem is, I've already phoned a dozen places, and every venue that can hold three hundred people is booked solid. I have no idea what to do."

"I wish our joint was bigger," Earl said, glancing around their cozy little room with its six tables, lace curtains, and wood-stained walls. "We could fit—what?—t'irty people in here if nobody breathes too heavy. Maybe t'irty-five if we stack 'em." He shrugged. "But if dere's anyt'ing we can do…"

Angie smiled. The three men had built this place with their bare hands—and a little help from her teaching the cook how to broaden is repertoire to more than spaghetti and meatballs, as well as some as decorating tips. The first time she'd walked in, she'd been drawn by the ethereal name, Wings of an Angel. She'd imagined white marble, harps, cherubs. Instead, she found three grizzled parolees, bad lighting, and gray Formica tables. She convinced them to swap in lace curtains and warm wood.

The name, she later learned, wasn't about angels at all, but an old song about a prisoner saying if he had the wings of an angel, he'd fly over the prison walls to freedom. So much for the ethereal.

"I know you'd help if you could, Earl. Thank you."

Before he could answer, the door swung open and Richie Amalfi sauntered in.

Although Richie was Angie's cousin, the two were as different as tiramisu and Twinkies. Angie came from comfort; Richie came from the streets. His father was killed when he was quite young, and he was an only child, raised by his widowed mother. Tragedy struck again four years earlier when his fiancée died in a car crash. That had sent Richie on a downhill spiral, drinking too much, eating all the wrong foods, and generally not taking care of himself until friends and family managed give him enough support that he was able to leave that long dark road and claw his way back.

Now, fast approaching forty, he was, to Angie's eye, quite handsome with soft, wavy black hair, soulful brown eyes, and standing fit and trim after straightening out his diet and exercising. On top of that, he was always impeccably dressed, sharing Angie's appreciation for good clothes and Italian shoes. She could tell from the cut that his gray sports coat was an Armani. With it, he wore a light blue shirt, no tie, black slacks, and buttery-soft black leather loafers.

He treated Angie as if she were the little sister he never had, and to her, he was the big brother she'd never had. She loved him without reservation. But to many others, he seemed a bit shady—probably because no one knew exactly how he made his money … and he made plenty of it.

He was often Angie's go-to guy when she needed something "fixed"—and she didn't mean mechanically. Richie always seemed to "know a guy who knows a guy" to take care of problems. Normally, she would have called him for help, the way she did about getting on La Maison Belle's calendar. But Angie feared that, this time, not even Cousin Richie's magic could help her out. Still, she couldn't help but smile and even feel a little relief to see him coming towards her.

He leaned down, kissed her cheek, and gave Earl a handshake. "Hey, Earl. Good to see ya. How about a glass of chianti while I see what's wrong with my glum cousin here?"

"Good luck," Earl muttered, scurrying off.

Richie slid into the chair beside Angie. "I heard. I'm sorry, Ange." He eyed her food. "That looks good."

"Here." She pushed the plate toward him. "I can't eat."

Earl returned with wine, sourdough, and silverware, skipping the menu entirely. Richie dug in while Angie caught him up on Bridezilla, La Belle Maison, and the looming disaster.

"So, lemme get this straight," Richie said between bites, twirling spaghetti with the ease of a man born holding a fork. "If Homicide clears the crime scene, the wedding's back on track. Otherwise? Fuhgeddaboudit."

She nodded miserably.

"My club's big enough," Richie said, "but it's booked Saturday for a Children's Hospital fundraiser. Not like I can throw sick kids out on the street."

"No, and I wouldn't let you. I just want La Belle Maison." She hesitated. "John Lodano said to tell you it's not his fault. What's that about?"

"Nothing." Richie's tone was too quick. "He's a friend, that's all."

Before Angie could press him, Richie's expression shifted. ""I understand Rebec—, uh, Inspector Mayfield, is in charge of the case?"

Angie's eyes narrowed. Something about the way he said (or, almost said) Rebecca's name was different.

"Yes. Why?"

He gave a half-shrug. "Nothin'. Just heard."

Angie pounced. "Did you know your mother phoned my mother saying you and Inspector Mayfield were getting 'too' chummy, as she put it?"

Richie groaned. "Ah, the Italian hotline. News travels faster than marinara on a white shirt."

Angie folded her arms. "So? Are you?"

He gave a sly grin that didn't reach his eyes. "That was a while ago. She's a cop. I'm … me. Oil and water. Don't sweat it, kid."

She rolled her eyes. "You could charm the pants off a saint, and you know it."

Richie nearly choked on his spaghetti. "Not the inspector, Ange. Trust me."

Her cheeks burned. "I didn't mean it like that!"

He chuckled, leaning back. "Relax, little cousin. Don't worry about Mayfield and me. We're just friends—or, kind of friends. She's a tough one, that's all I can say. But friends is good. Anyway, I'll nose around. See what I can find out. What's the bride's name again?"

"Taylor Redmun."

Vinnie's gravelly voice cut in. "Taylor?"

Angie and Richie glanced at each other, realizing Vinnie—and probably Earl—had been weaving around the restaurant and listening to their conversation.

"That's what she said," Richie spun around in his chair and eyed him. "Why?"

Vinnie moved closer, wiping his hands on a towel. Short, stocky, and bald, with bags under his eyes the size of carry-ons, Vinnie looked like exhaustion personified. "I wasn't listenin'—swear on my mother. Just happened to overhear."

"And?" Richie prodded.

"She useta come here," Vinnie said. "Sold us chocolate tortes we'd sell for dessert. Good ones, too. But mosta da money she made sellin' them to us went to food and wine. After a while, she stopped bakin' tortes, but still came by to eat and drink. She was always sayin' the cakes would be comin' soon. But they never did, and when she owed us over two C-notes in chocolate cake, we cut her off."

"What else do you know about her?" Angie asked.

"Cold fish, mostly. Could turn on da charm when she wanted, but nah, not a warm one. Yolanda down at the Blue Velvet Pub a couple blocks down Columbus knows her better. Worked wit' her. Cocktail waitress. She an' Taylor were tight. Heard Taylor got canned for doin' too much nose candy. Maybe true, maybe not. Alls I know is she stiffed us, da mooch!"

At this, Earl finally wandered over, cracking his knuckles like he was warming up for a fight. "Yeah, what Vinnie said. She owed us cake, owed us dough, owed us respect. You ask me, world's better off."

"Shut up, Earl," Vinnie grumbled.

Richie pushed back from the table, tossing down a thick wad of bills. He smiled at Angie. "C'mon, cousin. Let's go find a bar that still makes a decent Brandy Alexander."

Angie arched her brows, then grinned, suddenly understanding. "I know just the place."

With that, the cousins left.

* * *

He stood in the shadows across the street, watching the police van rumble away with the bride.

His bride.

The flashing lights cut across the buildings, slashing red and blue wounds into the gray cement walls before vanishing into the dark. Then silence fell, thick and smothering, leaving only the echo of the engine and the pounding of his pulse.

When the street settled back into stillness, he slipped across and into the apartment building, every step quickening, urgent. The thought of her with *them*—and what they were going to do to her—drove him forward.

Inside his apartment, the stench of grease, mildew, and rotting paper greeted him like an old friend. This was his kingdom. His throne room of squalor. And like every kingdom, it had its treasures. Only three mattered: the television, an aging laptop, and a faithful printer—a laser so he didn't have to keep ripping off Staples to buy ink cartridges. Those toners lasted forever. Reliable. Not like people, who betrayed, who lied, who *left*.

He guessed, if he were being honest—which he rarely was—the place was cluttered: stacks of papers he considered important that he'd printed off for safe-keeping; newspapers he'd picked up as he wandered the streets; warped and grease stained magazines not even doctors' offices wanted any longer; Styrofoam containers stacked like coffins. Even fast-food wrappers carpeted the floor in a kind of mad collage. Every so often, he'd get sick of the mess and throw everything into a black garbage bag, but right now, he was glad that feeling hadn't come over him for at least two or three months. Maybe longer. Someday, he might pick it all up again. But not today.

A rat scuttled along the baseboard and vanished under the couch. He didn't mind except when he had to fight them for space on his sofa and bed. At least rats never turned up their noses. Rats never rejected him. Rats didn't laugh at him behind their little paws. They took what he gave and kept their mouths shut. He preferred them that way.

He crouched low and pawed through the paper stacks until he found what he sought: a neat stack of wedding announcements he had printed from the Chronicle's "Union Squared" page.

"Union Squared." Even the name was smug. He guessed it

was supposed to be some kind of pun on Union Square, once a clean tourist-and-shopper paradise in downtown San Francisco. The name didn't work at all for him. Too cute by half.

He hated cute. Cute was weakness. Cute was a mask people wore before they revealed the rot underneath. Weddings were the most disgusting kind of cute. A joke dressed in lace and champagne. And brides? Brides were the punchline. Dumb, simpering, painted dolls walking toward a future already doomed.

His hand trembled, curled into a fist. His nails dug crescents into his palm as his thoughts twisted back to the homicide detective. That smug bastard. He'd seen him before, too. Him and his fat buddy cop. They were at the bridal shop. Investigating that murder, he guessed.

It wasn't his fault. The woman should have given him the dress. He'd warned her. The dress wasn't worth her life. He knew that, but she didn't. Everyone always gave him whatever he asked for—that was the deal. Give and you go free. But instead, she screamed and ran. She might have had a gun hidden in there—how was he to know? He did what he had to, for self-defense.

And now, the same damned cop who'd been looking into that murder turned up here. He was the thief who had ripped Shawnita out of his world, out of the warm shadows of their basement sanctuary. She had been his. *His*!

But even though she was gone, he was sure her presence would still linger near him. He knew it would. Just as, in the past, sometimes he could hear her voice—not words, exactly, but a murmur, a hum in his blood. A softness brushing his skin. She had understood him in a way no one else ever had. She had listened when no one else did. She had never turned her back. She had stayed. Loyal. Silent. Perfect.

Even death hadn't ruined her.

Maybe he'd been too hasty calling the cops about her body.

But he'd been all but certain she'd been seen, and if so, the safe thing—the prudent thing—was for him to call the cops, to report finding the body, even though he knew they'd take her and he'd be alone once more.

He remembered, as he watched the cop at the bridal shop, the woman he'd talked to. She wore an engagement ring—a beautiful ring, too. Not the cheap one Shawnita had worn. The way they'd looked at each other as they talked … they were engaged. He knew it!

Which meant that damned cop had a bride to be with each night while he suffered all alone?

Damn him! He took Shawnita. He'd drag her to the morgue, spread her open under fluorescent lights, carve her and pull her insides out. The thought made his throat burn. His fists and jaws tightened until he felt the warm taste of his tongue's blood.

But then an idea struck. A plan. A great plan. Oh, yes. He would honor Shawnita properly. He would keep her memory alive. She would never be alone, not really. Because soon, the silence of the storage room would be filled again—with breath, with beauty, with love. A new bride. His bride.

The cop's bride. Somehow, he'd find her.

With renewed purpose, he flipped through the *Chronicle's* wedding announcements. The aged sheets of paper whispered against each other like brittle bones as he carefully scanned each page. Wedding announcements had interested him long before he met Shawnita. Plastic smiles on faces looking into the camera. Most of them somehow managed to show expressions filled with hope for a bright future—a future that everyone knew was a farce. And bright? Hah. He liked to look at the announcements and laugh at all the stupid people in them.

Stupid people made him sick. The world would be better off without them.

Shawnita had been lucky. She'd never made it to the altar, so she didn't have to go through with the whole wedding charade, a charade that ended in more misery than anyone should have to bear. Joy was fleeting, only sorrow stayed, crushing a person under its weight. He had never married. He was too smart for that. One woman after the other had turned him down—thought they were too damn good for him. They were losers. He finally decided to spurn them all. Who needed a living bitch to make his life hell? The silent ones, they made coming home worthwhile. Silent—like his Shawnita.

One by one, he continued to go through the announcements. And then he found it. The one he wanted. The one that felt like destiny.

The Amalfi-Smith wedding.

He stared at the glossy photo. Angelina Amalfi. The bride-to-be's smile gleamed from the page, stupid with joy, teeth bared like she had everything and more. Happiness dripped from the image, false and bright. It made his skin crawl. Still, he traced her face with a fingertip, slow and careful, outlining the curve of her cheek, the tilt of her lips. So pretty. Prettier than Shawnita. Prettier than any of the ones he had considered, even dreamed about, before he found Shawnita.

He bent over the paper, inhaling it, imagining her scent. Sweet. Delicious. Frightened.

The text gave him what he needed: names and dates. He already knew her car, her license plate. Finding her home would be simple. Easy. A little patience. A little hunting. He had always been good at hunting.

Saturday. Just days away. Not much time, but enough to prepare. Enough to watch. Enough to plan.

He closed his eyes and imagined the storage room, empty and waiting. Cold, yes—but soon it would be warm again. Alive again. Filled with whispers and trembling and the kind of love only *he* could give.

The detective, in fact, should be grateful to him. He was going to save the man from years of nagging, of whining, of the hollow charade of marriage. He would peel away the lie of happily-ever-after and reveal the truth. One day, maybe, the cop would understand. Maybe someday, he would thank him.

And if not? Too bad.

Because the bride already belonged to him. She just didn't know it yet.

CHAPTER 12

hursday, 5 p.m. – 1 day 22 hours before the wedding
Angie floated out of the Blue Velvet Pub feeling surprisingly buoyant, considering the day had started with death, disaster, and her wedding reception in jeopardy. A Brandy Alexander had helped. Brandy Alexanders always helped. Cream, chocolate, booze—if God ever invented a cocktail that counted as both dessert and therapy, that was it. She could almost forgive the universe for throwing murder into her wedding week. Almost.

Richie, of course, had ordered a gin-and-tonic "minus the gin," which Angie thought was simply called tonic water, but Richie claimed he was mostly on the wagon these days—or, at least, cutting back the hard stuff. To his credit, it had kept him alert enough to turn on his charm with Taylor's old roommate, the cocktail waitress with unfortunate taste in both clothes and gossip.

Once the woman learned Angie was "only" Richie's cousin and not his girlfriend, she warmed right up to Richie's smile. Angie watched in a mixture of awe and mild nausea as the woman practically melted into his flirtatious banter, and began pouring out information about Taylor that Angie was sure she wouldn't have shared with a grand jury. Angie prayed to every saint she could think of that Paavo never used this same technique in his interrogations.

When they finally left, Richie had the woman's phone number scribbled on a napkin (with lipstick hearts, no less), and Angie had enough intel to go to Paavo with her head held high. She wished Richie luck—mostly because someone had to, given his track record with women—and drove straight to Homicide, fueled by a mixture of cream liqueur and righteous determination.

As she drove, she found that after she and Richie learned more about Taylor, she actually felt better about the chance of having her wedding reception at La Belle Maison. But she also had to continue to attempt to find a back-up location, just in case. She knew her sisters as well as her mother were working on finding one, but so far no one was having any luck.

The homicide bureau was nearly deserted, just a few lamps glowing over desks piled with papers as Angie walked in. The only living soul was Inspector Luis Calderon, and calling him *living* was generous. Calderon looked like a man who'd been personally wronged by life, love, and laundry. His divorce had curdled him, leaving him sour enough to turn milk by glancing at it. Angie had once seen him glare at a Valentine's Day bouquet in the break room until the roses wilted.

She approached. "Excuse me."

After a long, theatrical pause, Calderon lifted his gaze. "Oh. It's you. Again. He's not here."

"So I see." She offered her brightest smile, the one that worked on waiters and, once, on a tax auditor. "Do you know if he'll be back soon?"

"I don't keep his schedule." And back down went his head, like she wasn't worth the energy.

Angie forced herself to remain pleasant. "Is he, by chance, working on the Taylor Redmun murder?"

This time Calderon moved slow as molasses, sliding the report aside, and regarded her with a face so long and tortured he could've been cast in a movie about the Great Depression. "Last I heard, he's on a different case."

Angie's stomach dropped. "No! Really? But … but who's helping Rebecca with Taylor's murder?"

"Rebecca has a partner, you know." His eyebrows twitched, which Angie suspected was his version of a belly laugh.

Her nose wrinkled. "So I've heard." Her pride warred with her sense of justice, but finally, in a rare moment of betrayal to her own ego, she blurted, "I think Paavo would help her solve the case a whole lot faster than a partner whose main thought is which fishing hole he'll go to when he retires!"

Calderon's eyebrows inched up again—possibly a record for him—and then, to end the conversation, he dropped his gaze back to his report.

Dismissed.

She huffed her way back to her car. Normally she tried not to phone Paavo when he was out in the field because it meant he was working a case—looking at the crime scene, interviewing witnesses, or whatever. He didn't like to be interrupted unless it was an emergency. And she respected his work. Mostly. But this —this qualified as an emergency. As she drove off, she told her car system to phone him.

When he answered, his tone was clipped. She opened her mouth to spill everything, but then her brain caught up: this was *not* a good time to tell him about her afternoon. Did she really want to admit she and Richie had gone rogue and played junior detectives? No. Not over the phone. For one thing, he'd be irritated that she didn't simply pass along Bridezilla's roommate's name to him or Rebecca. Actually, she would never have given the name to Rebecca.

So instead she went with the oldest trick in the book. "I'm just feeling bad I didn't see you last night," she said in her softest, most tragic voice. "I couldn't go on without talking to you..."

There was a long pause. She could practically feel him reading her mind, weighing her words, sensing the lie like a bloodhound. Finally, he said he'd come by her apartment after work, and she realized he was too busy to question her—at the moment. It was nice, she decided, that they both understood each other so well.

It was a victory. Small, but she'd take it.

She hung up, reminding herself—again—that this was the life she had chosen. Wife to a homicide inspector. Late nights. Missed dinners. Cancelled plans because someone inconveniently got murdered. That was Paavo. That was justice. And damn it, that was the man she loved. Even if sometimes she wanted to strangle him with his own tie when he prioritized corpses over canapés.

Still, she reminded herself, he had been the one who worried about marriage more than she did. He was the one convinced he wasn't right for her, that she was too pampered and, yes, even too spoiled by her parents, to live with his grim schedule and his brooding moods. She, on the other hand, had almost never doubted. Almost. Eventually, she had convinced him. And now, the wedding was nearly here.

Which was when the universe decided to throw her another brick.

Her phone rang. Caller ID: *Wholly Matrimony*. At last. She'd left a message for Chef Maurice earlier about a possible venue change and expected him to phone back hours ago. Relief bubbled in her chest.

"Hello!" she sang out, bright as a bell.

"Miss Amalfi?" The voice was female, sharp, weary.

"Yes."

"This is Linda Withers. I'm Chef Maurice's assistant and business manager."

Angie's relief bubble burst like a pressure cooker with its jiggler ripped off. Her gut clenched. Something in the woman's voice whispered doom. "Yes?"

"I'm afraid I have some terrible news."

No, no, no. Angie tightened her grip on the wheel. "Yes?" she squeaked the word again.

After a moment, Ms. Withers continued. "Chef Maurice isn't here, and ... I don't think he'll return by tomorrow night for your dinner on the cruise."

Angie's throat closed. "But—he'll at least be back for Saturday's reception dinner."

A pause. Too long.

"Well ..."

That was it? Angie couldn't take it any longer. *"What are you trying to tell me? Of course he'll be back! I have three hundred people expecting foie gras and soufflé! Where the hell is he?"*

The woman sniffled. "Miss Amalfi, I'm sorry. The truth is, we don't know where he is."

"You don't *know*? How can you not know? Is he missing? Dead? Have you called Missing Persons? CNN? Put out an Amber Alert? I'll call my fiancé—he'll unleash the whole department! This is terrible—Maurice could be in danger!"

"Please, it's not what you think." Another sniffle. "Our business hasn't been doing well. We have creditors. Too many. And people these days want raw, vegan, tofu, gluten-free—anything but good, rich, calorie-filled, sauce-enhanced French cuisine. So ... it's just a guess, mind you, but ... but ..."

A sinking feeling struck; Angie feared she knew where this was going. She stopped at a red light and didn't even care when the light turned green and the car behind her started honking. "Out. With. It."

"He's absconded with what little money we had left. He disappeared. I think the check your father gave him to pay for the reception dinner—I mean, a fancy French meal plus wines for three hundred people, not to mention the Friday night meal —was simply too much temptation. He took the money and ran."

"No!"

"So it appears."

Angie suddenly felt so dizzy she put the car in drive and somehow, pushed her way onto the right hand lane, and pulled into a bus stop where she stopped. She didn't care if a bus flattened her. She cared only about one thing: her wedding was collapsing.

"You've worked with him," she whispered desperately. "You know his recipes. And your kitchen staff is still there to help. You can put on the dinner. It might not be as perfect as Chef Maurice would have made it, but it'll be delicious, I'm sure."

"You haven't quite understood everything I've said." Ms. Withers sounded on the verge of tears. "We have no money left. No money to pay me or the staff for the work we've already done last week for a different wedding reception. No money to buy the food or the wine, let alone to pay for the time of the sous chefs, dishwashers, waiters or anything else."

"The business took my father's money!" Angie wailed, tears and heart-attack threatening as the image of her three hundred guests picking at rotisserie chicken and vegan kale chips filled her head. "The wedding is the day after tomorrow! You can't do this to me."

"I'm so sorry." Linda's voice cracked. "But as of today ... there's no longer any such thing as Wholly Matrimony."

CHAPTER 13

Thursday, *7 p.m. – 1 day, 20 hours before the wedding*

Seven o'clock at night, Homicide was nearly silent. The bureau's overhead lights hummed faintly, casting long shadows over the empty desks. Only Rebecca remained, hunched at her computer, scrolling through notes and trying to untangle the conflicting stories she'd gotten from the Redmun-Borden wedding party.

She heard footsteps—deliberate, cocky, impossible not to notice—striking against the tile floor. She didn't need to look up. Only one man walked like that.

Richie Amalfi.

He always strutted. Or swaggered. Or sauntered. Never just *walked*. And she hated that. Hated the way her stomach always tightened when she saw him.

"I thought I'd find you here," he said with a grin that was pure trouble.

Rebecca's first thought: *Hell.* Her second: *God, he looks good.* Which she hated even more. The other inspectors had warned her about him—don't get too close, don't trust him. He had too many "friends" with rap sheets, too many shadows trailing behind him. Even Paavo, who usually had a clear handle on people, admitted he didn't quite know what to make of Angie's cousin.

So why did her pulse kick up a notch every time he leaned too close?

"Could this day get any worse?" she muttered, frowning at him. "Oh, right. Yes. It just did. What do you want, Richie?"

He dropped into the chair across from her desk, far too comfortable in a place he didn't belong. His smile widened. "Rebecca Rulebook. You really know how to make a guy feel welcome."

She rolled her eyes. That damned nickname. He loved tossing it at her like a dart, and she hated that a part of her—some rebellious little shard—almost liked it.

He pulled out his phone and turned the screen toward her. "I came to show you this."

She leaned over, refusing to notice his scent—something dark and expensive with a reckless edge. "Fascinating. Angie in a bar. What's your point?"

"Not Angie," he said smoothly. "The cocktail waitress with her. Yolanda Herrera. She and Taylor were tight. Roommates, even, for a little while. Angie and I talked to her. She had a lot to say."

Rebecca's head snapped up and then she jumped to her feet. "You *what*? You went nosing around in my murder investigation?"

He leaned forward, reached out, and took her hand before she could snatch it back. The touch was warm, firm, and far too intimate. For a split second, she forgot to breathe.

"Sit," he said softly, tugging just enough that her knees threatened to buckle. His voice—smooth, low, sinful—melted into her like warm butter on toast.

She yanked her hand away and stayed standing, her glare sharp as a blade. "Don't tell me what to do."

"Hey, I wasn't nosing," he said, leaning back, stretching out like he owned the place. "I was keeping my cousin company. You know Angie—once she's set on something, she's not stopping. I figured better me having her back than her walking alone into something stupid and maybe dangerous. And, between us, she was never going to come running to you with whatever she found out."

Rebecca's heart kicked again when his heavy-lidded dark eyes caught hers. God, those eyes. She hated how they could pin her down, make her feel like she was the only woman in the room. The only woman anywhere.

"Fine," she said finally, sinking into her chair. "So what's this supposed to mean? Am I supposed to be thrilled?"

"Overjoyed," he said with a slow grin.

She clenched her jaw. That grin was lethal.

"Taylor liked to put on airs," he began. "But she was going nowhere but downhill, and fast. She liked snorting coke, even lost her job at the Blue Velvet because of it. But then she met Leland Borden—steady job, nice guy, and absolutely head over heels that a woman who looked like Taylor, and with dreams of becoming a movie star, should have any interest in him whatsoever. She wanted to move in with him, to let him support her. But to her amazement, he actually wanted to marry her."

"So she found a sap, big deal." Rebecca folded her arms, still managing to frown at him.

"Around the same time, she heard about a movie holding auditions in the city—the director and producer live here. She looked into it. It's apparently some cheap-ass, half sci-fi, half soft-porn thing about horny steel-eating creatures from outer space. To her, it was going to become the next *Star Wars*. Anyway, she landed a small part—about three lines with lots of screaming and showing lots of skin—but then she heard a bigger role was opening up. That was when she decided to throw a wedding that would impress the people putting on the movie, the producer, director, and all the money men.

"She got Leland to agree to put up the money for La Belle Maison. Keep in mind, he doesn't have that much either, but he'd do anything for her. He was afraid if he said no, she'd walk. So he said yes, even though it together with the rest of the wedding and the rock she wanted on her finger, nearly wiped out all his savings."

"Unbelievable," Rebecca murmured. No wonder no one liked the woman.

"But true. I had my cell phone on record as Angie and I talked to Yolanda. I'll email a copy to you. There's a lot of background noise, and lots of extra chatter like you've got to do to get people to open up and tell you what they really think. But I'm giving you the gist of our thirty or forty minute conversation."

"You got her to talk that long?"

"Sure. It was easy. The Blue Velvet wasn't that busy. And, she, uh, liked talking to me."

Rebecca's jaw tightened. The image of him when he was flirting, turning on the charm, the way he could look at you with those bedroomy eyes and smile as if you were the most wonderful person in the whole world, suddenly came to mind. She hated those memories, and told herself that there was something about Richie, even when he was being helpful, that absolutely rubbed her the wrong way.

But, maddeningly, there were other times …

"Okay," she said, trying to keep her mind off the man, and concentrating on the helpful information he'd found out. "Send me the recording and I'll look into it."

"Hold it," he said. "You haven't heard the best part."

He said nothing until she lifted one eyebrow. That was as much as she'd ease up to let him know she was interested.

It did the trick, and he continued, "After she did that, booked the big space, invited some fifty important people from the film, only a few showed up. Most of the guests were Leland's family and friends. She didn't even invite Yolanda, her supposed best friend, even though Taylor had confided in her all along about everything."

Rebecca just shook her head at the complicated lives some people lived—and died living.

"Also, Yolanda said that the women Taylor asked to be her bridesmaids weren't asked because they were her friends. They weren't. They were chosen because they were involved in the film industry but not on camera. In fact, they weren't very good looking, and that way Taylor would look even prettier for the movie bigwigs she'd invited—who hadn't bothered to be there."

"What a bitch!" Rebecca shouldn't have said that about her victim, but she couldn't hold it in any longer. Professionalism be damned.

"Exactly," Richie said with a grin that she'd loosened up a bit.

"So …" Rebecca drew in her breath. "If all this is true, and I'm not saying it is or isn't at this point, then it's very likely not the bridesmaids or filmdom guests I should concentrate on, but maybe I need to look more closely at Leland's family and friends—and maybe at Leland himself." She faced her computer again. "I should get back to this."

Richie nodded, then stood. "Have you had your dinner yet?"

"No," she said quickly. "And I'm not hungry."

"You've got to eat," he pressed, voice dipping again, too persuasive, too damn intimate. "Come on. Something quick. We'll even eat in the car, if you want."

His offer was so, so tempting. But she shook her head, clinging to her professionalism like a life raft. "No, really."

He gave a half-smile, slow and knowing, like he could see right through her. "All right. I'll head to the club. But, Saturday…"

She barely glanced up at him. "Saturday?"

"Paavo's wedding."

She turned back to the computer. "I don't think so. I'm not

one for weddings. I'll probably still be working on this case. Hopefully wrapping it up."

His gaze met hers and held a long moment; he wasn't smiling, but was measured and serious. "The wedding is at three p.m. I'm in the wedding party and have to get there early or I'd pick you up myself. Saint Peter and Paul's Church. Be there."

He wasn't teasing, and she felt as if something hot, unspoken, and perhaps dangerous pulsed in the space between them.

And then he abruptly walked away.

Rebecca sat frozen, staring at the emptiness he'd left behind. She should have called after him, should have told him she wasn't going to any damn wedding. But her throat was tight, her pulse was racing, and her body betrayed her with the one truth she couldn't admit.

She wanted to see him again.

CHAPTER 14

Thursday, 8 p.m. – one day, 19 hours before the wedding

Angie had been phoning the Never Sea-Sick Cruise and Events Charter since she got home that afternoon. Every call had ended the same way: a chirpy answering machine message that was starting to sound smug. By the tenth try she was ready to strangle whoever had recorded it. But Angie was desperate. If any place in San Francisco had staff on hand at night, it was a cruise charter. Boats didn't send themselves out; someone had to wave bon voyage and make sure the tipsy passengers didn't fall overboard before they even left the dock. And someone had to oversee the kitchen to offer food and drinks.

By eight o'clock she'd had enough. If the Never Sea-Sick people wouldn't answer their phone, she decided to march down there herself and demand answers.

The pier was alive with its usual evening chaos. The tang of salt and diesel hung heavy in the air, mixing with the smell of fish from restaurants and vendors along the street. Harbor lights winked on the water, rippling and scattering into dizzy reflections. Gulls wheeled and screeched overhead, clearly hoping someone would toss them a French fry. A boat just returning from a harbor tour unloaded its passengers—tourists clutching cameras, seashell necklaces, and plastic cups with straws curling like antennae.

Angie found the charter office easily enough: a squat, flat-roofed building that looked like it had been designed by someone who once saw a postcard of Miami Vice and decided to wing it.

To her amazement, the door was locked. *Locked?* She banged on it and rattled it like a mad woman, then ran to the dock just in time to watch another charter boat pull away, strings of party lights twinkling, a band thumping out a muffled rendition of "Sweet Caroline" while passengers cheered.

Tomorrow night, the one cheering was supposed to be her. Her wedding party—on one of those very boats—sailing off into the night like glamorous cruise people. She clung to the thought like it was a life preserver.

At least boats were stable. In theory. She gave a nervous laugh at the irony—cruise charters might keep her wedding afloat as long as half the passengers didn't end up clinging to paper bags at some point.

She was about to lose hope when a man and woman strolled toward the office now that the boat had left.

Thank you, Jesus! She thought as she dashed toward them, nearly tripping on a coil of rope. "Excuse me! Excuse me!"

The woman squinted at her. Angie explained who she was, and that they needed to talk. One of them was Jessica Lenz, the cruise director she had spoken to on the phone a number of times. Jessica invited her inside.

Angie had imagined a cruise director as someone glamorous, all nautical stripes and chic sunglasses. Instead, Jessica was big, broad-shouldered, and looked as if she could wrestle a marlin into submission. Her blond ponytail was yanked back so tight it looked painful, her pale eyes seemed unimpressed, and her whole aura screamed: *You're annoying me already.*

But she unlocked the office and waved Angie inside.

The interior was trying very hard to be a boat. Wood-paneled walls and ceiling, plank floors, and—because subtlety wasn't on the decorator's radar—a stuffed swordfish leaping eternally from above the receptionist's desk. Coils of rope, bits of tackle, and generic ocean art filled every remaining space. The whole thing smelled faintly of varnish and lemon Pledge, as if covering up a darker undertone of mildew and fishiness.

Angie perched on the edge of a chair in Jessica's office and blurted it out: "I know I told you I didn't need your company to cater my dinner tomorrow night. But something terrible has happened."

"Sorry to hear that," Jessica said flatly, as sympathetic as a DMV clerk.

"My caterer folded," Angie rushed on. "I just got the call. They've gone broke, shut down, disappeared. Poof. I'm left with nothing."

Jessica's eyebrows crept upward like seagulls catching a thermal.

"I'm going to have thirty people at the dinner." Angie's voice climbed an octave. "Thirty hungry people! I was hoping your staff could help."

"On a Friday night?" Jessica barked a laugh. "We told all the kitchen people they weren't needed. That *you said* they weren't needed. So most of them found other jobs. And to prepare a special meal, which I expect you want, requires time."

"I know, but I'm desperate. I need to feed them something. *Anything.*"

Jessica folded her arms, thinking it over. "I could try," she said finally. "But it'll be a skeleton crew. Definitely not our best.

The only thing we could serve on short notice is roasted chicken."

"Chicken?" Angie almost whimpered. Why was she cursed with chicken? Rubber chicken haunted every bad banquet hall memory she had.

"Even then," Jessica went on, "there's a twenty percent surcharge. We'll need to scare up people who know how to roast chicken and make mashed potatoes and succotash."

"Succo—" Angie broke off, hyperventilating. Succotash. The most hateful dish in the history of sides. Mushy corn. Weird lima beans. The flavor profile of punishment. If Chef Maurice hadn't vanished, she'd kill him for leaving her stranded like this.

"Can we work out something—" she tried.

"Take it or leave it. I mean, it'll be a miracle if I find a staff who knows how to do more than boil water."

Angie shut her eyes, praying for divine inspiration.

Jessica shrugged. "Or, you know, there's always thirty Happy Meals. They even come with toys." She burst into hearty laughter at her own joke.

Angie gasped. She pictured the little red boxes lined up like caskets on the buffet table. Her, dressed in the beautiful outfit she'd carefully chosen for a dinner cruise, handing out plastic-wrapped cheeseburgers and soggy fries.

She wanted to storm out, but desperation caused her to swallowed her pride—and her palate.

"I'll take it." She licked her parched lips. "The chicken and … whatever vegetable you can muster."

He watched the petite woman leave the cruise ship office and march toward her BMW, her heels clicking against the pave-ment with a sharp rhythm that cut through the night air. She moved quickly, as though pursued by her own thoughts, unaware that something far more interesting than a bay cruise was awaiting her.

And he noticed, even more than he had the first time he saw her, that she was a truly attractive woman—her features exotically Mediterranean, and also somewhat delicate. Just the way he liked his women. Even more than he'd liked Shawnita, whose looks were a bit large and crass, even when she was alive. Not that it had mattered that much to him ... or to her.

Once he had found this one's name in the newspaper, learning more about her had been laughably easy. A little digging online, a scroll through Facebook, and there she was—posing outside her apartment building like she was handing him directions. She all but posted a blueprint of her life, and he had studied it obsessively.

Earlier that evening he had gone to her apartment, and stopped his car next to a fire hydrant as he studied it. His fingers drummed the cracked steering wheel as he tried to figure out what it would take to get inside her apartment—lockpicks, or maybe just waiting for her to buzz herself in.

But then fate rewarded him. Out of the garage shot a gleaming BMW, all smooth lines and smug paint, and at the wheel, as if delivered to him by providence, was Angelina Amalfi herself.

He followed her without hesitation.

She drove like a woman trying to outrun her problems, weaving through the streets with reckless abandon. He kept two cars back—twice running a red light to do so—his heart pounding at the adventure she was giving him, and all the while thrilled by her defiance, by her fire. She finally stopped at a pier. She got out of the car and ran to the water's edge. The night around her seemed restless—the slap of waves against pylons, the mournful cry of a gull, the wind rattling a loose sign overhead. She looked fragile there, yet brimming with purpose. She looked so alone there. Was this the time? He was about to move when he realized there were simply too many people around getting on and off the boats.

Angie turned away as a boat left the pier. *Now,* he thought, *go back to your car, Angie ... and I'll be there for you.*

But then another woman—big, commanding, a Valkyrie in jeans—showed up. Angie joined her and together they slipped into the charter office, swallowed by its shadowed doorway.

Her took a deep breath. This wasn't a setback. It simply gave him more time to prepare.

He eased out of the Chevy, pressing himself behind a telephone pole. The wood was splintered, sticky with years of staples from forgotten flyers. From here, he had a clear view of her car. His heart quickened. This kind of opportunity didn't come twice. No crowds. No witnesses. Just him, her, and the dark swell of the bay.

His hand brushed the knife in his back pocket. The hilt was warm from being carried all day, and when his fingertips settled on it, he felt calm, powerful. Yes—this was the right place. This was the right time. He could end her pre-wedding misery. She'd never make it down that aisle.

At last, the door of the office opened. She emerged, not drifting dreamily but striding, fierce and focused. He almost laughed at the fire in her step—God, how he adored her spirit! He could barely wait to see that spirit tremble, break, surrender.

She raised a remote, and her BMW chirped in response. Lights blinked, the engine coughed awake. That was when he knew he had to hurry. He quickly realized she wasn't one to spend time looking in her visor's vanity mirror to check her make-up, or to carefully fasten her seatbelt so as not to wrinkle her clothes, or to do heaven only knew what else many women did, all the while leaving their driver's side door wide open or, at least, unlocked. She wasn't the kind to dawdle. That made it harder for him.

By the time he moved, she was already in the driver's seat,

her hand curling around the door handle. He lunged, stretching out his arm. His fingertips brushed the cold metal, almost there, almost—

The door slammed shut.

White-hot pain exploded through his hand as two fingers were caught by the unforgiving frame. He bit back a scream but couldn't stop the strangled cry that tore from his throat. The agony was blinding, sharp enough to make him stagger. He yanked his hand free before the bones flattened, but the damage was done. His fingers throbbed, grotesque and swelling, the skin already darkening.

He doubled over, gripping his hand with the other, stamping his feet in an ugly dance of pain. Tears welled unbidden, stinging his eyes, trailing down the grime on his cheeks. He never cried. Not when his father had beaten him. Not when his mother had died. But now, because of her—because of *her*—he was sobbing like a child.

He jammed the injured fingers into his mouth, sucking them as though that could erase the pain, as though he could swallow the humiliation. Straightening slowly, he glanced toward her car...

She was gone. Oblivious. She had sped off into the night, not even glancing at the strange man flailing inches from her door, not hearing his cry of pain, not feeling the danger that had nearly wrapped its fingers around her.

He stood there trembling, blood roaring in his ears. She had escaped this time. But she couldn't escape forever.

What could she possibly have been thinking about? Certainly not her surroundings, not that she was all alone out here, and certainly not about him.

And that ... *that* was her mistake.

CHAPTER 15

Friday, 10 a.m. – 1 day 8 hours before the wedding

That morning, Angie felt as if she'd been run over by a freight train, the kind that carried not only coal and cattle, but also her sanity. First came the twin disasters of Chef Maurice absconding with her reception money—who knew chefs moonlighted as con artists?—and then having to serve her Friday night wedding party chicken and succotash. Succotash! A side dish so pitiful, it sounded like something prisoners in Alcatraz might have been forced to eat. If that wasn't an omen for Saturday's meal, she didn't know what was.

The only thing not yet ruined was her beautiful wedding cake—assuming the bakery didn't spontaneously combust, collapse into a sinkhole, or get taken out by a meteor. At this point, all three were distinct possibilities.

The one tiny bright spot in her otherwise dismal existence was Paavo's arrival at her apartment around ten p.m. last night. He'd told her he and Yosh were finally pulling together solid evidence in their cases, narrowing everything down to one killer. Which, in her book, was great—except Angie knew what Paavo *really* meant: they'd make it to the honeymoon for sure, but he'd still be taking phone calls about strangulation patterns and blood-spatter analysis while enjoying the beaches of Kauai. She could see it now: two lovers, alone in a moonlit cabana, the scent of orchids in the air ... *ring-ring.* There goes the romance, as she wrestled the phone out of his hand and flung it into Mauna Loa ... which wasn't on Kauai but at this point, she didn't care.

Before she had to start plotting volcanic phone disposal, she'd switched the conversation to Taylor Redmun-Borden's murder. She finally confessed to Paavo how she and Cousin Richie had met with Taylor's so-called best friend, Yolanda Herrera. Predictably, Paavo bristled, ready to lecture her about meddling in homicide investigations, but then—miracle of miracles—he didn't. After a quick call to Rebecca Mayfield, during which he discovered Richie had already beaten him to the punch, Paavo left Angie blissfully unlectured. Truly, it was the most unexpected gesture of their entire courtship.

At six a.m., he went home to shower and report to work, while Angie, desperate for the mythical "beauty rest" all bridal magazines promised, crawled back to bed. Except sleep, like the perfect wedding reception, eluded her. Finally, she gave up, staggered to the kitchen, put on coffee, and opened the front door for her freshly delivered *San Francisco Chronicle.* She had re-subscribed only last month, just to make sure her wedding announcement made it into the paper a month before the wedding, even though she'd missed the ridiculously early deadline. Really, who *decides* that true love must be reported before Tuesday at 3 p.m. at least six weeks before the wedding date? Did Cupid keep office hours?

She yawned, stripped off the rubber band, unfolded the paper, and shuffled toward the coffee pot—until her eyes locked on a headline at the bottom of the front page.

At first, she thought the words were blurred from sleep-deprivation. But no. They were crystal clear.

Never Sea-Sick Cruise & Events Charter Company Busted!

"Noooooooo!" Angie screamed, louder than the headlines, louder than a foghorn on the bay.

On shaky legs, she carried the paper to her petit point sofa and collapsed with a thud. The article was worse than the headline. DEA officers had conducted an undercover sting and found several employees smuggling heroin. Heroin! Who even used it anymore? Weren't these the days of cocaine and fentanyl?

For the cruise, she'd ordered champagne, hors d'oeuvres, and a string quartet—and what she got was a floating narcotics ring. As a precaution, the DEA had shut down the entire operation at eleven p.m. last night. Her reception venue was officially closed.

So much for "happily ever after." At this rate, she'd be lucky if her reception ended up as a half-eaten sheet cake in the church's parking lot.

Still half-asleep, with no caffeine in her system, Angie called the Never Sea-Sick office, hoping against hope her boat would still sail that evening.

The phone rang and rang. No answer. Not even voicemail. It was as if the entire company had been swallowed by the Bermuda Triangle.

The next thing she knew, she was curled up in the fetal position on her sofa, whimpering softly into a throw pillow. She pictured herself in her wedding gown, leading her guests in a reception conga line … straight into a police lineup.

Finally, unable to stand her own pitiful sobs, she called her mother. Her sisters had stopped answering her calls days ago, no doubt screening her out of sheer survival. But Serafina picked up. Bless her.

"Come see me, Angelina, now," her mother ordered in that tone Angie knew better than to argue with.

And so she dragged herself upright, clutching the newspaper like Exhibit A in the case of *The Universe vs. Angie Amalfi.*.

He was ready for action. Furious. Ready to kill.

He'd put on overalls and rummaged through some business cards people had given him over the years until he found one that should work, and drove straight to Angelina Amalfi's apartment building.

The overalls fit him like armor. Under his arm, a folded tarp. Hanging from the tool loop, the hammer he'd chosen for her. He had the plan rehearsed: a card from the Salvation Army to fool the doorman that he was there to pick up a donation, a quick knock at her apartment door, one hard swing, and Angelina Amalfi would be nothing but a rolled-up carpet he could haul to his car.

After circling the Russian Hill neighborhood for forty-five maddening minutes in search of a legal spot—he didn't dare risk a ticket that would put his name in police records—he finally found one four blocks away. Too far. Inconvenient. But she couldn't weigh that much.

He patted the tarp, grinning as he walked. Soon. Very soon.

When he finally reached her building, sweat dripping down his back from the brutal climb—he had no idea streets in this area were so steep—he was nearly trembling with anticipation. One more turn, one more step, and she'd be his.

But then he froze.

A white Mercedes SUV swung around the corner, tires squealing, horn blaring at a jaywalker who jumped out of the way.

Then the SUV braked hard in front of her apartment building. Two doors popped open, and two women spilled out, chatting, laughing, fussing with their coats. Her sisters—he'd see pictures of them as he researched Angie Amalfi on the internet.

What the hell?

And then, there she was—Angie—stepping out the apartment building's main door, waving to them, and calling out something he couldn't hear. The three of them clustered together on the sidewalk, arms linked, radiant with that easy, familial joy.

His fingers twitched around the hammer. Three against one. But if he moved fast—

Then fortune tilted his way.

One of the sisters got back into the driver's seat, while another dashed back into the apartment building, pulling her phone from her purse, and telling Angie to "wait here a sec."

Angie lingered by the curb and began searching in her tote bag for something. For one precious moment, she was all alone and distracted.

His pulse hammered. This was it. He slid the tarp under his arm, angled toward the curb, and started forward, a wide, fake smile pasted on his face like any other worker approaching a client's door. She didn't even look up. One more step, one more breath—

A horn blared. He jumped and turned his head to see what was happening.

The sister in the SUV had decided to get out of the car and swung open her door without looking, causing an approaching driver to hit his horn, hard. Angie, startled, leapt sideways— directly into the killer's path. She bumped his arm hard enough to knock the hammer free from his overalls, and she almost fell, but caught herself in time.

For an instant their eyes met. Hers widened, confused, unsettled. She gave him the once-over—the overalls, the tool belt, the tarp—and her brow furrowed as he bent to scoop up the hammer.

"Sorry!" she blurted, half-apologetic, as the sister inside the building ran out, grabbed her arm, and the two hurried to the SUV.

And then it was over. The other sister, properly chastened by the near miss, had already started the car, and almost immediately, they drove off.

He stood frozen on the sidewalk, his fingertips burning red with fury, the hammer handle slick with sweat. So close. So close. If not for that damned SUV horn, she'd have been his.

But then he shook his head. Whatever was he thinking? Her sisters would have been witnesses. The only way to stop them from going to the police would have been to capture them all—maybe by threatening Angie with the hammer if they didn't follow his orders.

He grinned at the idea. He'd always liked the idea of a harem.

His smile vanished. He didn't want to get too big about himself. He needed to be cautious, to plan much more carefully. He headed back down the steep sidewalks to his car, still remembering the echo of her perfume as she nearly fell into his arms.

He saw it as an omen for things to come.

CHAPTER 16

Friday, *Noon – 1 day, 3 hours before the wedding*

"You've got to hear these kids," Yosh said as he led Paavo to a flat across the street from the project where the dead bride had been found.

Earlier that day, the medical examiner had contacted them. She had managed to pull enough fingerprints to identify the victim: Shawnita Hickman. She'd been picked up a few times in Los Angeles for possession of drugs, disorderly conduct, and misdemeanor theft. She'd been booked, but then let go, and no charges were ever filed.

Paavo queried the police records and found a missing person's report filed on her in Los Angeles. He called the detective who had the case, and the detective filled him in on the details.

Shawnita Hickman was known to hang around with the "899" gang there. When last seen, she was on the way to her outdoor wedding in a park with Latrell Cruz, a gang member, when the two got into a fight. She slugged him, he slugged her back, and she ran off in her wedding dress. She was never seen again.

Her friends looked for her, but couldn't find her. Four days later, a sister went to the police and filed a missing person's report. The sister believed the 899s had killed Shawnita for dissing Latrell by leaving him at the altar, such as it was. The police investigated, but could find no evidence of a murder or anything else. Not that they tried particularly hard, and not that the people they interviewed were particularly cooperative. The LAPD concluded that Shawnita must have realized her life was in danger and had run away. They assumed she would eventually be picked up on another drug arrest, and that's how they'd find her. That was usually the way these cases went, the detective said. But that "next drug arrest" never came. Instead, she'd resurfaced on a filthy bed in San Francisco—dressed like a bride, decomposing.

Shawnita's disappearance had taken place four months earlier, and now, the M.E. believed Shawnita had been dead at least four months.

The day before, Paavo and Yosh had interviewed the people who lived across the street from the project as well as every tenant in the building where the "bride" had been found. Nobody had seen anything, nobody had heard anything, and nobody admitted to giving a note or having any contact at all with the building manager. All lies. Their silence only confirmed the inspectors' working theory: the building had secrets, and everyone inside it wanted to keep them buried.

Still, no physical evidence had turned up. Nothing at all had turned up, in fact, until Yosh saw a woman in the window of the flat he now brought Paavo to.

Entering now, Yosh introduced Paavo to the boys' mothers. When Paavo and Yosh had questioned them, they knew nothing. But things had changed overnight.

They had called Yosh to come inside to hear the story the boys had told them. They almost hoped the story wasn't true—

the result of too many scary movies on Netflix. But in case it was true, it was something the police needed to know.

Yosh put a gentle hand on each boy's shoulder as he introduced them to his partner. "This is Trevor, age 12, and his best friend, Jamiel, who's 11. Boys, this is Inspector Smith."

The boys looked wide-eyed at Paavo. Both wore baseball caps turned backward, sweatshirts two sizes too big, baggy jeans sliding off their hips, and worn-out sneakers with holes in the toes. They tried to look tough, but the way their eyes darted between Paavo and Yosh betrayed their nerves.

"Why don't all you boys sit down here and have a nice talk," Jamiel's mother said, indicating the sofa and chairs in the small living room. "Me and Kenda will head on into the kitchen and put on some coffee."

With the women out of the room, Yosh turned to the boys. "Tell Inspector Smith what you told me."

The taller one—nervous, chewing the inside of his cheek—spoke first. "I was curious about the blacked-out window in that apartment building. Didn't look right. So, one night, I decided to check it out. I didn't wanna steal nothing, just look. I pulled out the nails, used a slim jim to pop the lock. Took me a while, but I did it."

He stopped and glanced at Yosh, then at Paavo, uncertain.

"Go on," Yosh said gently. "You're not in trouble. Just tell him what you saw."

Trevor swallowed. "I peeked inside. And … I saw this woman lying on a bed. She was dressed like a bride. White dress, veil and all. But she wasn't moving. I swear she wasn't breathing. It was creepy as hell, so I shut the window fast and ran."

His hands trembled on the table as he went on. "I told my bro here, but he didn't believe me. Said I must've been seeing rags or something in the dark. But I couldn't get it outta my head. So, the next day, we went back."

The shorter boy—Jamiel—nodded, his Adam's apple bobbing as if the memory made him sick.

The tall one continued. "This time it was daytime. The lamp in the room was on, too. We saw her. For real. A woman in a wedding dress. Still on the bed. Still not moving. Her veil had slipped back, and her face—" He shuddered, eyes wide. "Her face was all mashed up, like it had melted or been crushed. It didn't look like no living person. But that wasn't the worst."

Jamiel spoke for the first time, voice breaking. "She wasn't alone."

Paavo leaned forward. "What do you mean?"

The taller boy's voice dropped to a whisper. "There was a guy. Lying right there with her. On the bed. Like … like he was holding her." His throat worked as he swallowed hard. "He was on top of her. His hands … on her. Like … like he was—"

He couldn't finish.

Jamiel shook his head violently, his cap slipping sideways. "It was sick, man. She was dead, I know she was dead. And he was actin' like she wasn't. Like she was his … his girlfriend or something." His voice cracked, and he pressed his fists hard against his eyes. "We just ran. We didn't even stop to close the window. Just ran."

Paavo sat very still. "Did you recognize him?"

Both boys shook their heads, pale beneath their bravado.

"All I know," the taller boy whispered, "is he was white. That's it. But I wasn't sticking around to see more. No way."

The silence in the interview room was heavy. The boys shivered, huddled close together, as though the memory alone was enough to make them want to bolt.

When Serafina put the word out that Angelina was having yet another meltdown over her wedding plans, two of her daughters—Bianca and Maria—dropped everything, drove across town, and scooped Angie up like she was a runaway teenager in need of a rescue. Their destination was, of course, Serafina's house, which had long been the headquarters for every Amalfi crisis, big or small. Already there, waiting, were the other two sisters—Frannie and Maria—each with their own brand of "help."

One look at the entire flock gathered for her, and Angie promptly burst into tears. "I can't do it," she sobbed. "I give up. My wedding is a complete failure. We'll have the ceremony, thank everyone for attending, and then send them all home. Paavo and I will leave early for our honeymoon. Unless a typhoon hits Hawaii. Then I'll drown and finally be free of this misery."

"Don't be ridiculous," Serafina said firmly, though she hugged her daughter tight. A short, well-rounded woman, she was wearing her favorite polka-dot dress that only served to emphasize her cheerful girth. She led Angie straight into the kitchen, the Amalfi war room, and sat her down at the big table. Before Angie could protest, her mother slid a steaming cup of coffee in front of her and a plate covered with enough iced Italian cookies to feed a platoon.

Normally, those cookies could calm any storm. Today, Angie looked at them as though they'd been baked from cement. She sipped the coffee anyway—sugar and caffeine being her only remaining allies.

"We'll figure something out," Bianca said. The eldest daughter was dressed like she'd come straight from a PTA meeting—straight dark hair to the chin, a blouse that screamed practical, and makeup that could best be described as optional. She was the family's voice of reason, which in Amalfi terms meant she was the one most likely to get ignored.

"No." Angie sat up straighter, her tears giving way to drama. She took a deep breath, squared her shoulders, and declared with queenly finality, "I know when I'm defeated. I have tried everything. This is a disaster. My wedding day will be remembered only as The Reception That Wasn't. From this day forward, when anyone speaks of Angie Amalfi, they will say, 'Ah yes, the woman who couldn't feed her guests!' I give up."

"Don't be silly," Caterina interrupted with a flip of her bleached-blonde hair. Cat, as everyone called her, was skeletal thin and dressed like she was going on a date with an LA casting director. "I was just reading the other day about a tornado in Kansas that flattened a wedding chapel. Flattened. Right after the vows. The couple had to sign their marriage certificate in a Red Cross shelter. And in Chicago, a toy drone flew into a wedding and scared all the guests so bad they trampled the cake. And—oh!—at a wedding in Florida, the food spoiled and gave everybody food poisoning. Now those are memorable weddings."

"Job's comforters would love you," Angie muttered, glaring at her sister.

Cat only shrugged, entirely pleased with herself. "So don't you dare give up. It could be a lot worse. At least your guests aren't puking in the parking lot."

"Not yet," Angie said darkly. "Cancel it. I don't have a choice."

"We always have choices," Maria intoned, her voice slow and serene, as if she were about to start chanting in Sanskrit. Maria wore her usual costume of jangling silver and turquoise jewelry, and her hair—a black sheet that nearly reached her waist— looked like it had been brushed 500 times already that morning. She was the "spiritual" sister, but if Maria started in with words about searching for the right path and doing whatever was "best" in life even if it wasn't necessarily what one most wanted to do, Angie was sure she'd slug her.

Angie was a God-loving, God-fearing Catholic, and she

loved her sister, but Maria's holier-than-thou attitude some-times pushed her over the edge.

Now, Maria pressed her fingertips together in some yoga-guru pose and added, "The universe always opens a door when another one closes. Sometimes the door is tiny, but—"

"Sometimes it's nailed shut," Angie snapped.

Maria ignored her. "I read just yesterday about a wedding in Bangladesh where wild dogs ran through the reception and made off with the buffet. Isn't that beautiful? The dogs ate, and the guests learned humility. What is one ruined wedding recep-tion compared to such profound lessons in compassion?"

Angie dropped her head into her hands and ground her teeth hard enough to make the whole table flinch.

"Honestly," Frannie broke in, rolling her eyes. Nearest to Angie in age, Frannie was also the sister Angie found the most irritating. "There are no wild dogs in San Francisco, no torna-does, and the only thing that's likely to stampede here is the cable car. Angie's wedding is indoors, the food isn't spoiled, and the only real disaster is her attitude."

"Very funny," Angie said flatly.

"Remember," Frannie went on, smug now, "Seth and I had a very simple wedding ceremony. Just family. No big fuss."

And look how well that turned out, Angie thought, her lips pressed shut. Everyone in the room knew Frannie's marriage was a soap opera with no commercials.

"Look on the bright side," Bianca offered cheerfully. "At least all this happened before Saturday. That gives us plenty of time to fix it."

"Aaaarrrgh," Angie howled. Bianca's endless optimism was like a toothache you couldn't get rid of. Angie threw her head back toward the ceiling, raised her arms high in melodramatic surrender, and wailed, "All I wanted was one special day! That's all! Was that so much to ask?"

"What's important is that you and Paavo get married," Serafina said firmly, her black eyes brooking no nonsense. "Not all the frills. The frills mean nothing."

"But it's my wedding day!" Angie wailed again.

Serafina just shook her head, sighed, and muttered, "*Dio mio*, give me strength." She put her hands on her hips. "Listen to your mother. You concentrate on Paavo and your marriage. Sit down, stop your tears, and leave the rest to us."

CHAPTER 17

Friday, 1 p.m. – 1 day, 2 hours before the wedding

Paavo and Yosh decided to zero in on the white males in the project complex, guessing that whoever had stashed the body in the storeroom most likely lived there or somebody should have noticed a perfect stranger going in and out. They had a theory about who the killer might be, but so far, they had no evidence at all.

There were seventeen white males, ten living with a partner. They decided to start with the single men, and to look at who had a car over the past four months. Somehow, Shawnita had moved from southern California to San Francisco. If she didn't travel on her own—which was unlikely reading the missing person's reports from relatives—someone moved her, and most likely used a car to do it.

Whether she was alive or dead for that move was anyone's guess.

Paavo phoned the M.E., Evelyn Ramirez. She was in her office.

After explaining which case he was calling about, he said, "You found some cloth fibers in the victim's hair. Can you tell me more about them?"

"They're heavy—most likely she was lying on top of whatever they're from. It could be a thick blanket of some kind."

"Okay. I'll get CSI on it," Paavo said.

"They're already on it. Nick was curious when he heard about them. He'll probably be contacting you this afternoon sometime."

"Great, thanks."

As he hung up the phone, he couldn't help but think of a heavy blanket—something Shawnita was lying down on. If she was being forcibly transported, she could have been put into the trunk of a car. They often had what felt and looked like a heavy blanket or carpeting in them.

Which, he wondered, of the seven men they were first looking at, owned a car?

He told himself he was lucky not to have a nine-to-five job. If he did, he would never have had the time to shadow Angie Amalfi. She never seemed to stop moving—flitting from one place to another, her schedule unpredictable and infuriating. Hours of his life had been swallowed up just trying to keep track of her, and still she barely spent enough time in her apartment for him to work out a proper way inside.

Patience, he reminded himself, though the word tasted sour. Patience was for men with time. He had none left.

After what he'd seen with her sisters, he doubted she'd be left alone on the wedding day itself. That meant his window was shrinking, collapsing in on him like a trap. It had to be today ... tonight.

Maybe he would just kill her outright. It wasn't what he wanted—such a waste of a bride as pretty as she was—but at this point, he didn't see many other options. The clock was running out.

Once she'd gone off with her sisters, he'd guessed she would come back home eventually. She had to. Everyone came home eventually. And he'd be waiting.

Parking on Russian Hill was impossible, and he wasn't about to circle endlessly like some desperate amateur. Instead, he pulled into a narrow driveway with a clear, unobstructed view of the entrance to her apartment building. From there, he could watch. He kept the overalls on, the Salvation Army card tucked in his pocket, the tarp and hammer within easy reach. His little collection of tools. His guarantee that once the moment came, he wouldn't hesitate.

If a traffic cop came nosing around, or the homeowner wanted their driveway back, he would simply move along. Until then, this was his perch.

The real battle now was against his own body. Already his eyelids felt heavy, the hours of waiting gnawing at him, threatening to dull his edge. He gripped the hammer, hard, the bite of the handle against his palm a reminder.

He couldn't fall asleep. He couldn't miss her. Not now.

Every shadow that drifted across the street, every pair of footsteps echoing on the sidewalk made his pulse quicken. Somewhere out there, she was moving closer to home. And when she did—when she finally stepped through that door— he'd be ready.

It took barely an hour before Maria—of all people—managed to pull off a miracle and find a venue for Angie's rehearsal dinner that very night. Maria, who on most days carried herself with the quiet composure of a nun, still had a few unexpected connections up her sleeve. Her husband, Dominic Klee, was the opposite of her in nearly every way: a dashing, larger-than-life jazz musician with a past that included just enough wild living to keep stories circulating long after he'd supposedly settled down. Dominic had fans everywhere, and one of his most devoted happened to be the owner of the Lusk Street Restaurant, a trendy, upscale spot tucked near the Giants' ballpark.

The restaurant's private dining room—an elegant space with soft lighting, gleaming wood, and enough seating for forty—had been made available on short notice to Angie's wedding party. When Maria broke the news, Angie could hardly believe her ears. Relief washed over her, followed quickly by gratitude that left her momentarily speechless.

The Lusk Street Restaurant wasn't the boat cruise Angie had once imagined for this night—no glittering views of the Bay, no city lights reflecting on the water—but as she thought about it, this might be even better. The place had ambiance, sophistication, and a reputation for flawless cuisine. And compared to the near-disaster she'd nearly endured—serving dry chicken and limp succotash from what she suspected was a drug front—this was nothing short of a blessing.

Serafina exhaled loudly, as if she'd been holding her breath for hours. "At least tonight is settled," she said, her voice edged with relief. "Now, we can focus on the reception tomorrow. I've already got an idea, but I don't want everyone just sitting here waiting on me. I need some quiet to think, and the rest of you need to go home and get ready for this evening."

CHAPTER 18

riday 3 p.m. – 24 hours before the wedding
Once the sisters were outside the house, the two departing gave Angie a long hug before Bianca and Maria bundled her into their car and drove her back to her apartment.

Inside again, Angie sank into a chair, relief mingling with exhaustion. Although relieved about that tonight's rehearsal dinner had been salvaged, she was still overwhelmed at the thought of finding a caterer to prepare the dinner for her wedding reception. If she could get La Belle Maison turned over to her on time, all would be well once more. The thought that it was Paavo's co-worker who was holding up all her plans was beyond maddening. The most difficult part was that she couldn't rant and rave to him about "Rebecca Rulebook," as she'd heard her cousin Richie call the nit-picker.

For years she had dreamed of a "La Belle Maison wedding reception." It was supposed to be the crowning jewel of her Big Day. Now, it felt like trying to pick up a handful of jello.

She tried making another phone call to a caterer, but the sharp tone of the assistant who answered—"I already told you we're too busy"—made it clear her sisters had already exhausted every lead. Angie hung up, staring at the receiver, her nerves unraveling thread by thread. This was supposed to be the happiest week of her life. Instead, it felt like a storm she couldn't get out from under.

There was, however, one place where her heart always steadied. One place she knew could repair her mood.

She grabbed her purse and jacket and hurried to the elevator. It rattled its way down, pausing at the fifth floor for another passenger before continuing toward the lobby. When the doors finally slid open at the ground level, the other woman stepped out—only to stop short, frowning at the workman in overalls standing directly in front of the elevator as if he expected it had arrived for his benefit alone.

"Still going down," the woman muttered, brushing past him. Angie hit the close-door button quickly, unsettled by the way the man mumbled something and stood staring at her. He seemed familiar. She exhaled only when the doors slid shut again.

A few minutes later she was in her car, steering toward the house she and Paavo would soon call home.

Her apartment was fine—she loved it—but the house in Sea Cliff was special. It wasn't just a place to live. It felt like a promise, a shelter. Older, yes, but full of charm, perched on a prime piece of land overlooking the restless Pacific.

The house had history—a surprisingly dark history. Thirty years earlier, a young couple had been murdered in the backyard, a tragedy that had scared off most potential buyers. Whispers about hauntings lingered. Renters came and went, none lasting long once they learned the story. But Paavo, being a homicide detective, had dismissed it all with a shrug. To him, death was simply part of life.

And when it went up for sale and its history was disclosed, potential buyers fled. All of which meant Angie and Paavo were able to get a much nicer house in a much better neighborhood than they ever imagined they could afford. Paavo had refused to take any money from Angie's father for the house. After they decided to buy it, they used money from the sale of Paavo's home as their down payment.

For the mortgage, they got a loan at the bank where the father of Angie's long-time neighbor and good friend, Stanfield Bonnette, was president. As Paavo put it, for the first time ever, he found a reason to like Stan Bonnette. Angie had to chuckle at that. Paavo wasn't jealous of Stan—no one would be—but he knew that Stan had often suggested Angie drop Paavo and marry him. Not that Stan was in love with her; he was in love with her cooking.

And then, after all this wedding stress was over, on Sunday, Mr. and Mrs. Paavo Smith would fly to a honeymoon cottage far off the beaten path in Kauai. All Angie wanted was a place with no telephones, no crime, and where no one would interrupt their honeymoon. For once in her life, she wanted Paavo all to herself. She could hardly wait.

After spending a week there, when they returned, they would go to their new house. It was already furnished with a quite a few things, such as the new master bedroom set with a California king-size bed. Her queen-sized one, a bed she must admit had served her and Paavo well, would be relegated to the guest room. The day following that, the movers would pick up all her possessions plus Paavo's few belongings from his house —which would then be turned over to the new owners—and deliver everything to Clover Street. Her sister, Cat—who was a realtor, and also the one who had handled all buying and selling transactions involved—had volunteered to see that everything was moved properly into place.

And then, there, they would settle down. Just the two of them. Maybe.

Although Angie never said a word about it to Paavo, she had witnessed a number of strange occurrences inside the house and in its back yard. She had worked hard to explain them away, but still...

Most unsettling was the small white terrier who seemed to appear whenever she visited.

But despite all that, the more time Angie spent at the house, not only did the potential "ghostly" nature of the house not bother her, it was having an opposite effect—making her feel safe and welcome. The more she was there, the less the supposed haunting worried her.

When she stepped through the front door that evening and drew open the living room drapes, that same sense of calm swept over her. The worries of caterers and menus faded, at least a little.

She brewed herself an Americano in the brand-new espresso maker, a gleaming contraption installed in her freshly remodeled kitchen—a gift from her parents finished only five days ago. With cup in hand, she wandered into the living room, where a couple of folding director's chairs and a plastic table stood in for the furniture that hadn't yet arrived. Beyond the sliding glass doors stretched the deck, the lawn, and a six-foot high wooden fence that surrounded the back yard. Behind the fence was a small bit of land and then the cliff that dropped to China Beach. Although the doors were shut, the steady hush of the surf drifted faintly through the afternoon air, soothing her nerves.

That was when she saw a movement in the garden. There he was again: the little white West Highland Terrier, trotting toward the house to then sit neatly on the opposite side the glass. His intelligent eyes locked on hers, steady and unblinking.

"Well, hello again," she said softly, setting her cup aside to open the door.

At once he trotted in, heading straight for the kitchen where he knew she kept a stash of food for him. He was a curious creature. Though he seemed comfortable enough in her presence, he never let her touch him. The moment she reached out, he'd dart away—yet he never stayed gone, always circling back to sit nearby, observing her intently. As much as she longed to scoop him up and scratch behind those perky ears, she respected his boundaries.

He was well-kept, his coat snowy and soft, his eyes bright, his body sturdy and healthy. Not a stray, surely. And yet, when she'd asked around the neighborhood, no one admitted to ever seeing him. That in itself was unsettling, especially since Eric and Natalie Fleming, the murdered couple, had once owned a dog of this very breed. Could this little fellow be a descendant of theirs? Or something stranger?

Sometimes, watching him watch her, she wondered if he was more than a dog—if he carried with him some silent link to the past. A fragment of a spirit, perhaps. She pushed the thought away, reminding herself that ghosts weren't real. Everyone knew that. Still, she had caught herself more than once calling him "Jock," the very name of the Flemings' terrier, and the way he responded—ears perked, tail wagging—unnerved her.

She opened a can of a fancy organic dog food, a brand she'd picked out in the store only because its ingredients sounded wholesome enough for a person to eat. She spooned half the can into the porcelain dog bowl she'd bought just for him, set out a dish of fresh water beside it, and stepped back. Only then did Jock trot forward, tail wagging, eating as delicately as if he were a guest at a fine restaurant.

Afterward, he lapped at the water and padded into the living room, where he lay down on the carpet with his paws neatly crossed, gazing at her with an air of expectation, as if waiting for her to confide in him.

Angie laughed softly. She did love to talk. So she talked to him—about the wedding, the endless problems with the reception, even her ideas for more remodeling once she and Paavo moved in.

Jock listened, his head on his paws, his soulful brown eyes following her every word and gesture. It was uncanny, the way he seemed to understand.

And then, just as suddenly, his head snapped up. A low growl rumbled from his throat. He trotted to the sliding glass door, ears pricked, body tense.

Startled, Angie followed. What could he see, she wondered. When she opened the door, Jock barked sharply. "Go on, boy. Go get'em," she said and watched with amusement as his little legs raced across the lawn toward the back fence.

There were a couple of trees in need of pruning but a number of overgrown bushes on the property, especially near the fences. They were something else she needed to work on once she and Paavo were living there. Jock, as usual, scooted under the bushes and vanished from her sight.

Strange little guy, she though, and went back inside to retrieve her coffee cup.

CHAPTER 19

Friday, 3 p.m. – 24 hours before the wedding

As soon as her daughters left the house, Serafina Amalfi made herself a strong cup of coffee and gathered the untouched cookies they had left behind. She sat heavily at the kitchen table, staring at the plate as though answers might come to her from its surface. Her heart ached in a way that nearly brought her to tears. To see her Angie—her baby—so unhappy the day before her wedding felt like a wound carved on her chest.

She wished—oh, how she wished—her daughter could understand that a wedding wasn't about the trappings, the flowers, the music, or the food. Those things were just falderal, the silly little decorations of life. She loved that word, falderal, so close to *fardello* in Italian—baggage. And that was all it was. What mattered was the heart of the thing: two people, deeply in love, standing before God and their family, vowing to spend their lives together. And, God willing, it was also about the children who might come from that union and carry the family forward.

But Angie was young, full of dreams, and she had looked forward to her perfect day for a long time. Serafina understood that, too. How could she not? To Angie, it must feel like all her hopes were crumbling, every plan dissolving into ashes before her very eyes.

Still, some things Serafina could never understand, no matter how much she tried. Her daughter—her youngest, her precious girl—wanting to celebrate her wedding reception in a hall where a bride had been murdered? *Madonna mia!* The very thought caused a cold chill to run over her entire body! As if it weren't already bad enough that Angie was marrying a policeman—a man who walked with danger at his side every day. Serafina truly loved Paavo and welcomed him to the family, but she also lived with the fear of what his job might mean, and she knew that Angie, stubborn as she was, could not keep herself from being drawn into his world of blood and crime.

And then, to add to her grief, the two *testa dura's*— and she didn't care she'd just mixed the Italian words for "hard head" with an English plural "s"—went and bought a house where the owners had been murdered. *Dio mio!* Murdered in the backyard! It brought tears to her eyes to think about! Who would buy such a house? Beautiful or not, Serafina would never, *ever* live where death had left such a stain. Some things could not be scrubbed away with soap and holy water.

She sighed, pressing her hand to her heart. She would never understand her daughter.

But now—without Angie even knowing—Serafina had a chance to fix at least one thing. She could at least save the reception. Somehow, she would make it beautiful, joyous, and unforgettable.

Her mind turned over the string of disasters that had plagued the wedding plans, and she felt her skin prickle. Such relentless bad luck did not come naturally. Someone had surely given her daughter the *malocchio*—the evil eye. Some jealous person who could not stand to see the Amalfi family happy. Serafina's eyes narrowed. If she ever found out who had done such a thing, God help them, for they would pay. Still, the best revenge would be this: to pull off Angie's wedding reception and make it grander, more marvelous, than anything her daughter had ever dreamed.

And even if her practical daughters said there was no such thing as the evil eye, Serafina wasn't so foolish as to take chances. Life had taught her that unseen forces were everywhere, watching. She would not ignore them.

The thought drove her to her bedroom, where she opened the velvet case that held her favorite rosary. Sitting on the bed, she wrapped the beads tightly around her hand, the crucifix biting into her palm. She prayed, with all her heart, for Angie and Paavo—for their safety, their happiness, and that somehow this wedding would not be remembered for tragedy but for joy.

Then, as if heaven itself had whispered in her ear, the idea that had niggled in her mind earlier, came to her as a full-blown plan. The longer she sat with it, the more possible—no, the more *right*—it felt.

She sprang into action, making one phone call after the other to see if her idea was even possible. By the time she hung up the last call, her heart beat faster with a spark of hope.

But one hurdle remained: Sal.

Her poor husband. With his bad heart, she had tiptoed around him, careful not to upset him with too many bills or too much stress. Truth be told, some of the expenses for Angie's wedding would have given another man cardiac arrest. But Sal was stronger than she'd feared. Thank the saints.

Now, though, she would have to sit him down and tell him the truth: that the fortune already spent was, for the most part, gone. The food, the wine, the caterer—*pfft*, all wasted. The venue, perhaps a little refund, but not enough to matter. She would have to confess that everything had fallen apart.

And then—only then—could she tell him her plan.

A solution. Not perfect, not certain, but something. Something that might save her daughter's wedding day.

The only person she had not called was Angie. Her baby had been through enough. She could not burden her with hopes, not yet. First she needed to be sure this idea could be pulled off. Then, and only then, would she tell her daughter.

———

The call Paavo had been waiting for, finally came in.

"The fibers in Shawnita Hickman's hair were used to carpet a car's trunk," the crime scene unit tech reported. "Specifically, the carpeting was used in a Chevrolet Cavalier from 1995 through 2002."

Paavo didn't even need to look at the list of names to know who owned a Chevy Cavalier, only one man did. A 1998. He gave Yosh a grim nod. "Got him."

No sooner had he hung up than Evelyn Ramirez was on the line.

"I was just talking with CSI," she said. "Have they called you yet?"

"They did."

"Good. Because I've got one more piece for you. We managed to pull DNA off the victim, and I'm confident it belongs to the killer. The lab's backed up, but I've flagged it priority—you should have results within forty-eight hours."

"Perfect. But how can you be sure it's the killer's?"

Ramirez's voice dropped, edged with disgust. "Let's just say our guy didn't stop at murder. He went back. Again and again. Necrophilia. A whole lot of it."

She hung up before Paavo could respond.

For a moment he sat in silence, the words painting an image he didn't want. Then he exhaled, pushed it away, and looked at

Yosh. "Now all we need is Benny Simms—the manager. Let's bring him in."

CHAPTER 20

Friday, 4 p.m. – 23 hours before the wedding

Benny Simms narrowed his eyes as he followed Angie's car through the winding streets, his pulse quickening when she finally turned onto a stretch of road lined with large, elegant homes. A street sign read *Sea Cliff Avenue*. He thought he'd heard of that before—an upscale neighborhood where the rich and powerful tucked themselves away from the rest of the city. Not the sort of place his acquaintances ever went. Not the sort of place he belonged.

So what was *she* doing here?

When she pulled to the curb and stepped out, his surprise deepened. Angie didn't just *visit* the house—she walked right up to the front door, produced a key, and let herself inside. His heart gave a strange lurch. This was hers? This mansion on the edge of the world, where the earth dropped off into gray water and jagged rocks below?

She had moved here. Settled here. His bride.

And now, finally, she was alone. His heart raced as a smile stretched wide across his face.

He parked two streets over—yes, this area did have some street parking—and circled back on foot, hugging the shadows like a man stalking prey. When he reached the house, he continued past it. It was the last one on the block, and beyond was just the hillside and then a drop—the "sea cliff," he realized —to the Pacific down below.

He studied the area. The house sat like a fortress, ocean winds tearing at its glass windows. The fence that encircled the property stretched a good six feet high, tall and solid. He walked over to it and ran his hand along the boards as he paced the length of it, looking for a weakness—a gate, a loose board, anything to help him scale it.

Nothing. He walked along the side fence until it met with the fence that ran along the very back of the property. He saw that the back was where the fence edged the drop of the cliff, and protected *his bride* from straying too close to that edge and possibly falling to her death.

Wind whipped up the salt spray below, the sound of the crashing surf echoing in his chest like distant thunder. Beyond the back fence, his bride's property met her neighbor's, who also had a six-foot high fence.

Damn! There was no way around the fence. There was only one way: *over*.

He spat into his palms, then leapt, fingers scrabbling for purchase at the top of the boards. The wood bit into his hands as he clung there, pressing the soles of his worn tennis shoes against the boards to keep from sliding down. His arms trembled with the strain. Could he haul himself up far enough to swing a leg over? He wasn't sure. He wasn't as strong as he once was, years ago. But he had to try. He had to reach her.

From where he dangled, he could see only slivers of the house's roof. No windows. No sign if she was inside, or if someone else waited with her. His arms shook harder. Sweat ran down his back.

But his need burned hotter than the ache in his muscles. He pictured her there, delicate fingers brushing back her dark hair, her lips parting in a smile meant only for him. His bride. He would rescue her, cherish her—if only she didn't scream and fight the way poor Shawnita had.

Still, he let himself drop back to the ground, then flexed his shoulders and rubbed his hands, needing to catch his breath before trying again.

He shut his eyes a moment as the memory of Shawnita suddenly clawed its way back to him, as vivid as if it had happened yesterday. The way she had sagged in his grip after her groom's fist left her dazed. She had run from the groom and his gang, running and stumbling until dazed and sick to her stomach, she was out of breath. All he had wanted to do was to help her. But the foolish woman struggled against him as he dragged her to his car. Her cries had been shrill, desperate, drawing eyes. If the gang that her groom belonged to had heard her and then found her with him ...

The thought had scared him so badly he had no choice but to smash her head against the car, again and again, until she stopped screaming. She was still breathing, he reminded himself, as he put her into the trunk of his car. She would have lived, if she hadn't been so stubborn.

But by the time he was sure he was no longer being followed, somewhere between L.A. and San Francisco, he pulled off the highway and opened the trunk. Her chest no longer rose and fell. Even her skin had cooled.

And she had been his secret ever since. In San Franciso, after a few weeks of him doing all he could to keep the store room sealed off so the smell wouldn't get out, to keep cleaning her body and using bug spray on it so the maggots and such wouldn't turn her skin to soup, the smell went away, and the insects died.

And finally, she was his, completely his, until those damn kids messed up everything. He thought about ignoring them, but he knew that eventually they'd tell what they saw and then the police would come nosing around. The best thing he could do was call the cops and pretend he was the one who had discovered her.

Those stupid, stupid cops believed him. They believed he knew nothing about who she was, or how she'd gotten there. Idiots! He smiled at his own cleverness. But, he thought, an eye for an eye. Or in this case, a bride for a bride.

Angie would be his second chance—his second chance at love. It sounded like a romance novel.

He took hold of the top of the fence again and jumped up, cursing under his breath as he tightened his grip and tried hard to boost himself up. He managed to get high enough to see into the yard and the back of the house.

A sliding glass door rattled open.

For a moment he nearly lost his hold altogether. She stood in the doorway, sunlight glinting off her hair, her head tilted down as though speaking to something at her feet. Then he heard her voice—soft, playful, directed not at him but toward the ground.

"Go on, boy. Go get 'em."

Benny's heart skipped. *Who?*

His stomach twisted and he nearly slipped off the fence, so confused was he, wondering who or what she was talking to when he felt a sharp tug yanked at his jeans just above the shoe. His body jolted. He craned his head down—and froze. Nothing was there.

His breath locked in his chest.

His grip failed. He crashed backward into the dirt, pain jolting up his spine as he landed hard. For a moment he just sat there, stunned, clutching his throbbing hands. The silence pressed in around him, heavy.

But he *knew* he had felt something. Something had touched him.

He staggered upright, telling himself it was just a nail, a

sharp edge on the wood. His imagination. Nothing more. But even as he turned to try the fence again, a dog barked. He looked back to see a dog between him and the street.

It was small and white, but growled, its body rigid. Its eyes— cold, brown, unblinking—fixed on him.

He hadn't heard it approach. He hadn't seen it coming.

A shiver crawled up his spine, the hair rising on his neck. This was wrong. All wrong. He wanted to lunge forward, climb back up, get inside, *take her*. But something in him—something primal—whispered a warning. Not yet. Not now. Wait.

The dog padded closer, its growl sounding lower, deeper, bigger.

His mouth twisted into a nervous grin, though his voice trembled. "Nice doggie." He thought about kicking it, but something about it scared him so much all he could do was back away, even as the tiny beast continued steadily toward him. "Good boy. Go away, now. That's a good, good—*No!*"

CHAPTER 21

Friday, 4 p.m. – 23 hours before the wedding

Paavo and Yosh were in Benny Simms' apartment. They'd gone to arrest him, but both he and his car were gone. Paavo immediately sent out an APB on the Chevy and Simms, warning that he could be armed and dangerous.

In the apartment, they found Simms' newspaper clippings about the city's upcoming weddings—including Angie and Paavo's. On the laptop—he hadn't bothered with a password—they found pictures of Angie from her social media posts.

Paavo was beside himself when he realized what had to be going on in Simms' warped brain.

In an almost miraculously short amount of time, a call came in from patrol about the APB he'd sent. The yellow 1998 Chevy Cavaliers with dents in both front fenders stood out like a sore thumb in the tony Sea Cliff district. It was the land of BMWs, Mercedes, and even a Tesla or two or twenty. Not junks. Also, it was an area the SFPD made sure was well patrolled.

Paavo's stomach dropped like a stone when he heard the location.

It was only a block from Clover Street. From *their* house, his and Angie's.

A rush of heat flared through him, followed by cold dread.

He jabbed at his phone, dialing her number. The call rang once, twice, three times. No answer.

"Yosh, let's go," he said. "They found Simms' car. I'll tell you about it as we drive. Got to hurry."

Yosh grabbed his jacket and followed Paavo. This wasn't a time for questions.

Paavo's chest tightened as he got into the driver's seat of the Ford SUV they drove. He tried to remind himself—she often didn't hear her phone. She buried it in that oversized leather bag, lost among receipts, lipstick, heaven-only-knows-what. Sometimes she shut off the ringer altogether if she wanted quiet, or if she tried to nap.

It probably meant nothing.

But Paavo knew better than to trust "probably." He had seen too many families torn apart because somebody thought *probably* meant safety.

He forced his mind back to Simms—the corpse, the obsession. Maybe in his warped brain he'd thought of that poor girl as his "bride." Maybe now he wanted another, to replace what had been "stolen." And who better than Angie?

The thought almost gagged him. It wouldn't be the first time some sicko decided to go after friends, relatives, coworkers, lovers, of the person he thought was persecuting him. Who better than the bride of the person who took his bride away?

He slammed the emergency light onto the roof of the car and hit the siren. The wail split the air, a sound that always made his blood pump faster as he stepped hard on the gas. Yosh glanced at him, but didn't ask. The set of Paavo's jaw told him enough.

"Where to, partner?" Yosh asked.

Paavo's face was grim. "He's near my new house. And Angie isn't answering."

"You don't think—" Yosh started.

"Why not?" Paavo snapped. His voice was harsher than he intended, tight with fear. "An attractive bride-to-be. Alone. Distracted. The kind of woman who'd smile at a stranger on the street if he looked lost. That's Angie." His voice broke on her name, and he couldn't continue.

"She might not even be there," Yosh offered.

"Or she might be." The words burned like acid. "Why else would Simms be out that way?"

The drive blurred. Sirens, red and blue lights ricocheted off houses. With each block they passed, his heart pounded harder.

When they reached Sea Cliff, Paavo killed the siren and shut off the light. He didn't care where Simms' car was. He drove straight to Clover Street, straight to his house. His hands shook on the wheel.

And then he saw it. Angie's car in the driveway.

No other car around.

His throat closed.

He barely had time to cut the engine before a man came sprinting toward them, dragged along by a black standard poodle straining at its leash. The man's face was white with panic, his arms flailing. "Do you guys have a phone? Someone's got to call the police!"

Paavo was already out of the car. "We *are* the police," he barked, flashing his badge. "What's happened?"

The man stammered. "A body—down on China Beach. At the foot of the cliff, just beyond the fence. He must've fallen. There's blood. He's not moving. I—I couldn't climb down—"

But Paavo was already running, Yosh following.

They reached the cliff's edge, and Paavo forced himself to look down.

A body lay sprawled face-down on the rocks, blood pooling dark beneath the head. The build, the hair, the clothes—it was Simms. Paavo recognized the same filthy shirt from their last interview.

For one sharp instant, relief surged through him. If Simms was down there, maybe—

But relief curdled fast. Why had he been at the cliff in the first place? Had he tried to climb? Had someone chased him? And where was Angie?

Paavo leaned out farther, scanning desperately. His vision tunneled, searching the rocks below, dreading to see a woman's body lying broken near Simms.

But Simms was alone.

Still, the dread wouldn't loosen its hold.

Paavo turned back toward the house, remembering Angie's car in the driveway, innocent as a toy. A six-foot fence cut off his view of the house, the garden—the fence that separated the safety of their back yard from danger of the cliff.

But a fence might not stop a killer. He wanted to go to see what had happened, but the dread held him back. It was too much. Just too much.

"I'll take it from here," Yosh said gently. His hand on Paavo's shoulder anchored him, but only barely. "Go to the house. Find her."

Paavo froze, torn between duty, the desperate urge to see her, and mind-numbing fear.

Yosh's grip tightened. "She's all right. I know it. Now go!"

The words broke through the ice inside him.

Paavo ran.

His shoes pounded the pavement, his chest heaved. His hands fumbled at his pocket for his key, slick with sweat. He jammed it into the lock and flung the door open.

"Angie?" His voice cracked. "Angie! Are you here?"

No answer.

His heart rammed against his ribs. He bolted into the kitchen—her bag sat on the counter, abandoned, the leather strap dangling. His eyes locked on it, and the certainty hit him like a blow: her phone, with his missed calls, was inside.

She hadn't heard him. She hadn't answered.

He spun back into the living room, chest heaving, trying to think. His hand clawed at the back of his neck. Where? Where would she—

The sliding glass door.

He lunged toward it, yanked it open—

And there she was.

Sitting on the deck, turned toward the sea. She jumped at the sudden noise, startled, then smiled—*that smile*—that melted him every time. Bright, warm, unknowing. "Paavo! What are you doing here?"

The wave of relief that crashed over him so fierce it hurt, a love so sharp it felt like pain. He wanted to crush her against him, never let her out of his sight again. At the same time, he needed to shield her from the ugliness that had just brushed so close, especially today—one day before they were to be married.

"I was nearby," he managed hoarsely. He crossed to her in three quick strides, caught her in his arms, and held on tight, breathing her in.

"Is everything all right?" she asked softly.

He kissed her hair, her temple, her lips—kisses that told her what words couldn't. "Now it is," he whispered.

But she drew back, her eyes searching his face. "Something's happened."

He forced a grin. "No. No, nothing. Just wanted to see you." His voice was too light, false even to his own ears. He changed the subject. "So, what are you up to? Why are you here?"

They sat together on the bare deck, their legs dangling over the edge. It was only a couple of steps down to what would one day become a weed-free lawn-covered yard.

"Sometimes," she began, "over the past few weeks and months when things like our wedding arrangements turned complicated, and I felt as if I couldn't make one more decision, I would come over here and remind myself of what's really important. There's something soothing about this house, about its location on this point of land where I can hear the steady, eternal sound of the ocean. And, of course, it has my little doggie friend."

With that she stopped talking and looked around. "Hmm, he was here for a while. I guess he went home. Anyway, as I was saying, I've always felt welcomed here, as if it's a little haven. It sounds funny, but I feel protected."

"I didn't know that," he said, his arm around her shoulders. "And I'm glad you've told me. I was worried you'd feel isolated since I have to work nights so often. It's not like Stan is right next door."

"Oh. Well, there's something I need to talk to you about," she said with a small grin. "That small house across the street is empty."

"No. He didn't."

"You never know about Stan."

"I'm glad you like him Angie, but to me, he's a pain in the—"

"I know. But he's got a good heart."

Paavo heard the wail of police sirens growing louder, rolling toward them.

"All right, Paavo." Angie eyed him suspiciously. "What's really going on?"

He tried to brush it off, "Someone found a body."

"A neighbor?"

"No. Just some drifter wandering through, apparently. Nothing to worry about. But that's why Yosh and I were near. He's taking care of everything while I came to check on you."

Her eyebrows rose, but she wasn't fooled. She always saw too much. "So that's why you looked so worried when you came in."

"Well ..."

"Paavo, haven't I told you that you don't have to worry about me? I know how to take care of myself."

His gaze drank in each feature of her expressive face. "You're right. You do, and I know it." And although he wanted to protect her from the truth, the fear that had gripped him all the way here wouldn't release him. He looked at her—the woman he loved more than his own life—and said quietly, "Because I love you, Angie, I'll always worry. Always."

But soon, their sweet moment had to end as Angie reminded Paavo they had to get ready for their wedding rehearsal at the church—and that they finally had a spot for their dinner where he'd be eating something tastier than grocery-deli rotisserie chicken.

CHAPTER 22

Friday, 9 p.m. – 18 hours before the wedding
Rebecca met with the crime scene inspectors late into the evening, the fluorescent lights of the lab buzzing overhead like a reminder of her own frayed nerves. Their findings were both thorough and maddeningly inconclusive. They had lifted a number of fingerprints from La Belle Maison's kitchen and anteroom, but none matched any known criminals. The knife used to kill Taylor Redmun-Borden—gleaming, cruel steel—had plenty of smudged fingerprints, but all of them belonged to members of the kitchen staff. No intruder prints, no stranger's telltale mark. Just ordinary, expected traces, tainted and useless.

When CSI found a white cloth napkin crumpled beneath a table in the anteroom, they concluded the killer must have used it to pick up the murder weapon, effectively smudging away any useful evidence. Clean. Cold. Efficient. That detail chilled Rebecca—it meant planning, not a crime of passion.

They also believed the killer had to be a man, given the sheer force required to drive the blade into Taylor's back. Some women could certainly muster that strength, but looking over the female guests and bridesmaids, Rebecca doubted it. Most appeared—at least to her eyes—in pitifully poor condition. Flimsy arms, fragile frames, not a single one likely capable of plunging a knife so deep. Rebecca, by contrast, prided herself on making time for the gym, at least three hours each week. She thought about it now with a fleeting, guilty flicker of vanity—but quickly shoved the thought aside. This wasn't about her.

The wedding had employed a professional photographer, but fate had laughed at them. At the very moment Taylor was stabbed, his back had been to the anteroom. And worse—when he finally noticed the bride stumbling toward the cake, crimson staining her gown, he had been so stunned that he lowered his camera to gape instead of capturing the critical seconds. Rebecca had nearly wanted to shake him when he told her.

She collected every photo she could from guests' smartphones. Most of the attendees had been film people, but instead of documenting the reception, they had turned the cameras on themselves, chattering and laughing. No one had caught the anteroom. Useless, again. Still, sifting through those candid snapshots, Rebecca did uncover one small lead: the "missing" third bridesmaid Sally Lankowitz had mentioned. She appeared in the corner of one photo, outside on the deck, cigarette in hand, smoke curling like a guilty veil.

Cross-referencing timestamps, Rebecca found three men missing from both the professional photographer's last shots and the cell phone photos captured around the time of the murder: the groom, Leland Borden; his brother, Mason; and his best man, Darrel Gruber.

Of the three, Leland supposedly adored Taylor, though Rebecca had seen enough marriages to know love was never a guarantee of loyalty. And the spouse was often the prime suspect in a murder. But a groom, on the wedding day—that was another level altogether.

The best man, Darrel, hadn't liked her, that much was obvious, but he had been Leland's friend since boyhood. Did he hate her enough to destroy his best friend's life?

The brother, Mason, was the enigma. He barely knew Taylor, yet his thinly veiled dislike of her had been obvious. Then again, nearly everyone Rebecca interviewed had spoken ill of Taylor. Other than Leland, Rebecca couldn't find a single person who genuinely liked the victim. Not being a fan didn't make you a murderer—but it made the suspect list endless.

She ran her fingers through her hair in frustration, then pressed her palms against her temples as she stared at the scattered evidence glowing back at her from her computer screen. It was Friday night. Tomorrow by noon La Belle Maison had to be cleared for Paavo's wedding reception. If she couldn't release the venue, her name would be cursed in Homicide—not just for bungling a case, but for personally ruining her colleague's wedding day.

And Paavo had already carried more than his share. He and Yosh had just closed the Benny Simms investigation. The most chilling part was when she heard that Simms, twisted by delusion, had tried to replace his "bride" by going after Paavo's fiancée. He'd died trying.

CSI had combed the cliffside behind Paavo's new home, piecing together the final, grotesque moments of Simms' life. Fingerprints at the top of the fence. Scuff marks where his shoes had slipped against the wood. His footprints, strangely, walked backward, step after step, toward the edge of the cliff as if pushed by invisible hands. They found no evidence of anyone else nearby. No second set of prints. No sign of a struggle. The official ruling: suicide, born of madness.

Angie swore she had heard nothing other than a neighbor's small terrier that had barked and then ran to the back of their yard. But it was in no way big enough to harm an adult male. She was convinced the dog had dug a hole under the fence, hidden by bushes, that it scooted under so it could come or go at will.

The Simms case had ended neatly enough for Paavo and Yosh, but for Rebecca it only deepened her despair. Compared to their closure, she had nothing. Taylor's murder sat before her like a gaping wound, unhealed, festering. Every eye in Homicide was watching her. Everyone wanted answers.

And everyone had been invited to Paavo's wedding. Lieutenant Eastwood himself had granted the entire squad the afternoon off, a gesture so rare it had sparked jokes and cheers. They had been looking forward to the food, the dancing, the celebration of one of their own finally finding happiness. Now, all of that joy hung in limbo—because of her.

Because of her failure.

Whenever her partner, Bill Sutter, was asked to step in and ease the pressure, he shrugged, muttered something noncommittal, and vanished—to the men's room, to the coffee shop, anywhere but at her side, vouching for her. She was alone in this.

The guilt was unbearable. Rebecca sat there, the glow of the computer screen reflected in her weary eyes, and hated herself for being the one standing between her colleague and his wedding day. If she failed, she wouldn't just be disappointing her lieutenant, or her squad, or her own sense of duty. She would be breaking something sacred for Paavo and Angie— tainting what should have been a perfect memory with blood and bureaucracy.

She buried her face in her hands, breathed in deep, and then forced herself upright again.

Late though it was, she made her decision. She couldn't give up, not now. If the evidence refused to speak, then she would go back to the source. One by one, she would interview the three men again—the groom, his brother, the best man. Somewhere in their stories, in their silences, lay the truth.

And she would find it—because she had to.

That evening, the wedding rehearsal went off without a hitch—just as Angie had prayed it would. After weeks of planning, worrying, and scrambling to patch up disappointments, she half-expected something to go wrong. Yet here she was, standing in the hushed glow of the church sanctuary, the vaulted ceiling high above her, the faint scent of incense still lingering in the air. Her family and closest friends surrounded her; the wedding party moved in quiet formation at the priest's gentle instructions. And through it all, she held Paavo's hand. His palm was warm, steady, reassuring—an anchor in the swirl of her emotions. Every squeeze of his fingers seemed to say, *I'm here. We're in this together.*

As they stood side by side, listening to the priest and the office aide who oversaw the practical, secular details of the service, something shifted inside her. For so long, the wedding had felt like a performance she was preparing for—a role in which she was expected to shine. Every dress fitting, every florist meeting, every frazzled conversation with caterers had been part of a script. But here, in the quiet reverence of the rehearsal, the illusion fell away. This wasn't theater. This was real life. A vow made to last a lifetime.

Her throat tightened as she stole a glance at Paavo. He wasn't Catholic, but he had attended marriage counseling classes with her without complaint, even with curiosity. Somewhere along the way, he had confessed that he envied her faith—that he wished he could believe as deeply as she did, that her trust in something larger than herself gave her a peace he longed for. At the time, Angie had only smiled and nodded, knowing words like his were often the first step toward something greater. Now, remembering it here in God's house, her heart filled with gratitude for him. She felt his thumb stroke lightly over the back of her hand, a small, absent gesture, but one that sent warmth through her chest.

The rehearsal ended more beautifully, more movingly than she could have imagined. A hush lingered as they exited the church, as though the sanctity of the vows-to-be still hovered over them. As they walked out, Paavo leaned close, his breath stirring her hair. "You looked radiant up there," he murmured, low enough that only she could hear. She blushed, but the smile that spread across her face stayed with her into the evening.

From there, they swept into celebration at the restaurant Maria had miraculously secured. To Angie's delight, the place was vibrant but intimate, with flickering candles on the tables and warm wood accents glowing beneath golden light. Paavo kept his arm around her chair through the meal, his knee brushing against hers under the table, grounding her even when laughter and conversation swelled around them. Somehow, despite the crowd, the staff had managed to serve everyone nearly at once—and they had even allowed the party to order off the full menu. The clink of glasses, bursts of laughter, and the aroma of rich food lifted Angie's spirits higher still.

"If only everything tomorrow could go as smoothly as tonight," she sighed, standing with Paavo and her parents as everyone who would be in the wedding party, spouses, and a few others, began to drift out into the evening.

"It will, sweetie," Connie Rogers said firmly, sweeping Angie into a hug that was warm and strong enough to dissolve some of her nerves. Connie—divorced, tough, but tender-hearted— was her matron of honor, her best friend, and her rock. "Haven't we always found our way out of one crazy mess after another?"

Tears pricked Angie's eyes. She clung to Connie. "You can say that again. As long as you're with me, Connie, I know we'll make it work."

"And me," came a voice from behind. Stan, with his crooked grin, stepped closer. Angie had talked Paavo into making him one of the groomsmen, though Paavo hadn't needed much convincing.

"And you!" Angie laughed through her tears, pulling him into a hug as well.

Stan dabbed at his eyes dramatically. "I'll come by tonight for one last midnight snack raid. It'll be my final one in your apartment. I'll try not to cry all over your trousseau."

Angie swatted him playfully. "If you do, you'll show up to the wedding with black eyes, I promise you. Now behave yourself, and I'll see you later."

Paavo slipped an arm around her shoulders then, pulling her close as Stan walked off. His quiet smile said everything—how much he loved her, how amused he was by her friends, how proud he was just to stand at her side.

Soon, only her sisters and parents remained. Bianca nudged their mother. "Tell her."

"Tell me what?" Angie asked, narrowing her eyes.

Serafina glared at Bianca but couldn't quite hide her smile. "I wasn't going to say anything, but—fine. We've got something worked out for you. A surprise. If the reception doesn't go as planned, we've got a back-up."

Angie blinked in astonishment. "You do? Where? Who's the caterer?"

"Don't worry about it, Angelina," Serafina said, waving off her questions with a flourish. "You just think about being a beautiful bride for your handsome groom." She turned to Paavo, her eyes softening. "*Caro mio*, you make me so happy. I look forward to dancing at your wedding. And I will."

"But—but—" Angie sputtered, caught between gratitude and frustration.

"*Andiamo!*" Serafina declared, clapping her hands as if the matter were settled. "Time for all of us to go home. We have a big day tomorrow."

"And tonight," Frannie muttered under her breath.

"Tonight?" Angie repeated sharply.

"Nothing," Frannie said quickly, too quickly. "I just … need to figure out what I'm going to wear tomorrow, that's all."

Angie tilted her head, suspicion stirring, but before she could press further, Paavo slipped an arm firmly around her waist and gently steered her toward the door.

The night air was cool as they stepped outside, a soft breeze carrying the scent of the bay. Angie leaned into him, exhaustion from the long day making her body melt against his. He kissed the top of her head, lingering there, and murmured, "Don't worry about secrets or surprises. All that matters is us, Angie. Tomorrow, you'll walk toward me, and I'll be there waiting. Nothing else matters."

Her throat caught, but she nodded, pressing her cheek against his chest. The steady beat of his heart calmed her in a way no words ever could. She wasn't sure she liked all the secrecy swirling around her—her sisters whispering, her mother plotting—but Paavo's steady presence beside her was enough to quiet her mind.

Tomorrow would be their day. And tonight, wrapped in his arms beneath the moonlit sky, she felt certain that whatever came, already they were more than halfway to forever after.

CHAPTER 23

Saturday 8 a.m. – 7 hours before the wedding

Richie showed up at Homicide at eight sharp on Saturday morning, only to find Rebecca at her desk—alone. The bureau was silent, the kind of silence that pressed in on the ears. Even her useless partner was nowhere to be seen. Papers were scattered across her desk, coffee cups stacked like grim trophies, and her pale face bore the unmistakable signs of a sleepless night. She didn't even notice him at first, her eyes fixed on the piles of evidence as if sheer willpower could force them to give up their secrets.

"No luck?" he asked at last, setting a Starbucks cup down in front of her. A non-fat latte—her favorite. He'd made sure to remember.

The look of surprise that flickered across her face startled him more than her usual scowl ever could. She blinked at the cup, then at him, and instead of the biting remark he'd braced for, she whispered, "Thanks." Soft. Vulnerable. A sound that sent an uninvited jolt straight through him.

"No luck at all," she added, her voice roughened by fatigue.

Uninvited, he dragged a chair over and dropped into it. He didn't care if she told him to get lost—he wasn't about to leave her drowning in this case. She looked exhausted, shoulders tight, hair pulled back with none of its usual polish. Beyond frustrated, too.

From what he knew, she'd never faced one of these "locked room" type murders before. Rebecca Mayfield was a grinder—she'd always find another witness, another angle, another door to knock on until a case cracked. But this one had her boxed in. La Belle Maison had become a gilded prison of unanswered questions. CSI had swept every inch, every hallway and crawlspace, with a fine-tooth comb. Security cameras proved no outsiders had slipped in or out. Which left only one horrifying conclusion: the killer had been one of the guests, or worse, someone who should have been trusted.

"I'm going through everything again," she said, her fingers steepled against her lips, head bowed as though the sheer weight of the puzzle pressed it down. "Even the trash. I must have missed something. I've boiled it down to the groom, his brother, or the best man. But which one? I don't know. I've even got friends in L.A. digging into Mason Borden's past—Taylor spent enough time down there chasing film jobs, there might be a link. I keep hoping the phone will ring with something—anything."

Richie watched her. The weary slump of her body, the flicker of anguish in those sharp blue eyes. She wasn't just exhausted—she was shaken. For once, she hadn't even tried to fence with him. No sarcasm, no barbs. Just raw honesty. That unsettled him almost as much as the case did.

"Sounds like the others are leaning on you and Sutter pretty hard," he said carefully.

Troubled blue eyes met his. He hated seeing her this way. The two of them were so different, so much at odds in almost everything, he knew they could never be more than friends—if that. Still, for some insane reason, he liked being around her and kept finding reasons to see her. Since when had he become such a glutton for punishment?

"Sutter would tell the crime scene unit to open up the space in a heartbeat," she murmured, leaning back in her chair, massaging her temples. "He says the case will be solved eventually, and that's that. But I worry that some evidence might be destroyed. The CSI has a few more areas they need to check, mainly the basement. It's a long shot, but nothing else has worked."

She gave a weary sigh. "It doesn't help that I feel as if I'm letting everyone down. I'm close to solving the case, I'm sure, but I'm missing something. The killer wasn't a pro, so how was he so clever?"

"You're right," Richie said, leaning closer to her as if he might give her some strength in this. "He wasn't a pro. And I doubt anyone went to that wedding intending to kill Taylor. So what happened in that moment to push someone over the edge?"

Rebecca's eyes sharpened a little. "Exactly. Why did the bride go into the anteroom? Answer that, and we'll know who followed her—and why."

She straightened in her chair, took a sip of the latte, and reached for a handful of plastic evidence bags. They clinked softly together, filled with the odd detritus of a shattered evening. To Richie, it looked like junk. To her, it was the only language left to decipher.

She fanned the bags across her desk and faced Richie. She looked so beaten down he wanted to pat her shoulder and tell her everything would be all right, but he knew she hated that sort of thing.

"I've been over this pile three times already," she muttered. "I tell myself I missed something, but…" Her jaw clenched. "I don't think so."

"What's in them?"

"Dirty napkins, mostly. A few with names and numbers scribbled on them."

"Really?" He dragged his chair closer, so near their shoulders almost brushed. He caught a faint scent—hand lotion, maybe—or maybe it was just her skin. Clean, sharp, something he shouldn't notice but he did. And liked.

She pointed to a napkin in an evidence bag. "Those numbers trace to wannabe film people, the types who'd never kill anyone. Probably hookups that never happened once the murder shut everything down."

He nodded, rifled through a couple of the other bags, then paused, lifting one. "What's this?"

Rebecca took it, smoothing it flat on the desk. Typed words glared up at them through the plastic: TOAST, followed by bullet points.

"The best man's speech," she said. "Or reminders for it. He told me he didn't give it."

Richie skimmed the list, frowning. "Weird. Doesn't seem like any best man's toast I've ever heard."

"It doesn't?"

"Hell, no. The best man is nearly always closest to the groom, so his talk is often jokes about the groom. He'll usually tell at least one embarrassing or funny story, and then he talks about what good friends they are and how lucky the groom is that he actually found a good woman to put up with him. But this one? It's all about the bride. Her accomplishments, her talents. Barely anything about the groom. This is strange, Rebecca."

She frowned, studying the paper. "I'll admit I haven't gone to many weddings, but what you describe is the way I remember them."

"The best man actually admitted that he wrote this?" Richie asked.

"All he admitted to was that it was the speech for his toast and that he didn't give it." Rebecca's brow furrowed as she pulled the typed guest list side-by-side with the toast speech. "Same paper, same font and font size—but it's typical computer paper, a common font, so that might not mean anything. But still…"

"Still?" Richie asked.

For the first time that morning he saw a hint of the Rebecca he knew—the one who thrived on puzzles, who wouldn't let go until she had a firm grip on the truth.

Richie watched her lips press together as she thought. Lips he'd noticed before. Lips he shouldn't be noticing now. He dragged his gaze away, but not before a flicker of heat stirred in his chest.

She interrupted his wandering thoughts with a sharp, "It doesn't make sense. The best man made it clear he didn't like Taylor. He even hinted she was driving a wedge between him and Leland. So why write this glowing speech? No way. It doesn't add up."

Her eyes gleamed now, sharp and dangerous, a hunter's gleam. He smiled despite himself. *God help him, he liked seeing her this way. Too damned much.*

"Then you need to talk to him again," he said, trying to keep his voice smooth, modulated.

Before she could answer, the door banged open and Bill Sutter sauntered in, his smirk firmly in place.

"Well, well. Here I was feeling sorry for you, Mayfield, stuck here on a Saturday morning all alone, and thought I'd lend a hand. Guess I was wrong." His eyes flicked toward Richie with a sneer.

Rebecca sat up straighter, her energy returning. "Good. You're here. We need to call in the best man. I've got a few more questions for him, and I think Homicide is the best place to ask them."

Richie rose reluctantly. He didn't want to go, but he couldn't stay. "I've got things to handle this morning. You get this wrapped up by two, call me. And either way—come to the wedding. Even if not the church, at least the reception. I'll text you the location. Most of Homicide will be there. You should be, too."

"I don't know. Even if he confesses, I'll have a lot of paperwork—"

"Rebecca," he said, his voice low, determined.

She looked up, her gaze puzzled.

He hesitated, then added, softer, "If nothing else… come for Paavo's sake."

For a moment, she seemed even more puzzled. But then, out of the blue, she smiled. He'd told her before that she had a beautiful smile, but it still hit him like a sucker punch.

"I'll try," she said. "Especially if I can get La Belle Maison opened up for them. I'm … I'm actually feeling a little optimistic."

Richie forced himself to leave, but the warmth of that smile lingered long after he'd walked out the door—along with the ache of wanting more than he knew he should.

CHAPTER 24

Saturday, 2 p.m. – 1 hour before the wedding
Paavo was more nervous than he had ever been in his life. Not even walking into a dark alley after a suspect, gun drawn, compared to this moment. His palms were damp despite the crisp San Francisco air, and he found himself pacing the small courtyard behind the church like a caged tiger, trying to draw strength from the sunlight and the quiet. The city, for once, seemed to be on his side—the sky a faultless blue, the temperature mild, the breeze barely stirring. It was as if the day itself had dressed up for him, presenting perfection for his wedding.

And yet, inside, Paavo felt anything but perfect. His chest was tight, his heart a dull hammer with the thought that, an hour from now, Angie would walk down that aisle toward him to become his wife.

He wasn't the kind of man to show much emotion—not in his work, and certainly not in his private life—but deep down, this mattered more than he could ever say. The case, the chaos, the uncertainty of the last few days—all of it had nearly stolen this moment. And now here he was, one hour away from marrying the woman who had somehow become his center.

With him in the courtyard were his groomsmen. Yosh, the best man, stood by with his usual sharp wit and steady presence, doing his level best to keep Paavo from coming completely unglued, and the others hovered near—Inspectors Luis Calderon and Bo Benson, Angie's neighbor Stan Bonnette, her cousin Richie, and even Doc Griggs, who had made the long drive up from Arizona with his new wife, Lupe. All of them were trying to keep the atmosphere light. They laughed, they teased, but Paavo only half-heard them, his mind a whirl.

Then his phone buzzed in his pocket. For one wild second, he thought of ignoring it—this was his wedding day, after all— but his instincts never let him ignore a call, not after a career in Homicide.

"Don't even think about it," Yosh warned, catching the look in his eyes. "You are not going out on a call. I like having my head attached to my body, and Angie would remove it if I allowed you to leave the church grounds even for a minute."

Paavo gave him the faintest, humorless smile and answered anyway. "Rebecca, what's up?"

The group quieted instantly, watching as Paavo listened. His face, so often impassive, shifted with each second—first tense, then incredulous, and finally, profound relief. When he finally spoke, his voice was low, thick with something that almost sounded like gratitude. "Thank you. Thank you so much."

He slipped the phone back into his pocket and looked at the others. His sigh was the sound of weeks of strain finally cracking open. "It's over. Rebecca caught the murderer. He confessed. And La Belle Maison is open for business."

The groomsmen reacted like a dam breaking—exclamations of relief, laughter, and disbelief all at once.

"So, are you going to tell us whodunnit? Or are you going to make us wait until Rebecca shows up?" Yosh demanded.

"It was the best man ... Yosh," Paavo said, and despite the grimness of it, he couldn't help a slight grin at *his* best man.

"Oh?" Yosh said, picking up on the strangeness of it all. "Now, I can understand feeling murderous when involved in wedding dramas, but not to actually do it. What happened?"

Paavo had to shake his head. "Taylor—who apparently became known as Bridezilla for good reason—wrote his toast for him, word for word, and ordered him to read it exactly as she wanted—praise for her and only her. He refused. She harangued him, threatened him, and then humiliated him. It was the proverbial straw that broke the camel's back. He snapped. Said he killed her to spare his best friend a lifetime of misery."

Inspector Calderon let out a bark of laughter, though his eyes were sharp. "He only regrets he has but one bride to dispose of for his friend. That's his defense, huh? I don't think that'll play too well in court."

Even Stan, normally the joker, looked sobered. "That poor guy—the groom. To find out your best man murdered your bride 'as a favor'... whoa, that's spooky stuff, man."

Paavo nodded but kept his own thoughts to himself. He wasn't about to admit aloud how grateful he was that the case had broken today, before the wedding, before Angie walked down that aisle. He was glad he didn't have to say "I do" with the weight of Taylor's unsolved murder hanging over them. And he couldn't deny—Rebecca had come through for him, for Angie, for everyone.

"We've got to let Angie and the others know," Paavo said at last. His voice was steadier now, but the hint of emotion lingered under it. "I know I'm not supposed to see her before the ceremony, but I can call her. She needs to know her reception venue is open for business after all."

"Let me handle it," Richie said quickly, stepping forward. "There'll be arrangements to work out. You know her mother's been sitting on a back-up plan in case this didn't come through. Better I talk with them than you."

"That's right, Serafina's secret plan." Paavo had learned that the Amalfis liked to do things their own way, and if Richie wanted to talk it over with them, he wasn't about to interfere. He gave Richie a nod. "Okay. Go for it. If you're brave enough to step between Angie, her sisters, and their mother, I won't stop you."

The laughter from the group eased the last of the tension. For the first time all morning, Paavo straightened his shoulders and let himself believe that the worst was behind them. Or so he could hope. And despite all his years of keeping emotions under lock and key, he felt his chest swell with pride, joy, and more than a tinge of sheer terror at what was soon to happen. The truth was undeniable: this wasn't just another day. This was *the* day.

Richie was directed down the hall to the room where the bride was getting ready. He knocked softly, already feeling out of pGlace, and Bianca opened the door a crack. Her eyes widened when she saw him.

"You aren't supposed to be here," she hissed, as though his very presence might unravel the sacred bridal preparations.

"I know," Richie admitted, his voice low. "But I've got news about the reception. Big news."

For a beat, Bianca studied him, suspicion and curiosity warring in her expression. Then she shut the door firmly. The muffled sound of women's voices carried on the other side. After a moment, the door opened wide, and she gestured him inside with a sweep of her arm. "All right. But make it quick."

He stepped into what could only be described as the most female room he had ever entered in his life. It hit him like a wave—silk, lace, perfume, and powder. Clothes, particularly underclothes, were draped over chairs and the backs of sofas.

Makeup brushes and compacts littered the vanity. Hot curling irons had been carefully placed on the counter. A clump of what looked like curly brown hair—a discarded extension?—lay on a tabletop.

The air was thick with competing scents: floral perfumes, baby-powder talc, and hairspray, all accosting him until he was almost dizzy.

Angie, radiant in her bridal gown, stood at the center of it all, surrounded by a gaggle of women and a sea of rose-colored satin and silk. For one wild second Richie felt like he'd wandered into a forbidden sanctuary—a harem's inner chamber, perhaps—and the instinct to flee rose sharply in his chest. But he straightened his shoulders, and forced his gaze away from the feminine chaos as he took a deep breath.

That was when he noticed Micky. The boy sat alone in a corner, looking small in his ring bearer's suit, his solemn eyes following every movement in the room. Richie's heart softened. Micky was the son of Paavo's first partner in Homicide. After Matt Kowalski was killed, Paavo kept in touch with the boy, teaching him to play baseball, basketball, and soccer, taking him to ball games, and just spending time with him. Micky's mother, Katie, at the moment was helping Connie Rogers with her hair.

Richie crossed to Micky, crouched, and put a hand on his shoulder. "We guys have to stick together," he whispered.

Micky gave him a quick grin and nodded, visibly relieved to have an ally in this sea of tulle and chiffon.

Only then did Richie straighten and address the women. His throat felt dry. "Rebecca Mayfield caught Bridezilla's killer," he announced. "It was the best man. Rebecca contacted La Belle Maison. It's no longer a crime scene"—he paused, watching Angie's eyes widen—"and they'll be able to have the room ready for the reception… if you still want it."

The effect was instantaneous. The room fell utterly silent, as if someone had cut off the music.

Angie gasped and then shrieked with joy. "Oh, my God! That's wonderful!" Her whole face lit with relief, her hands flying up as if she might clap in delight. But then, as the echo of her excitement faded, she realized she was the only one celebrating.

Her sisters exchanged uneasy glances. "That's great, Angie," Connie murmured, then suddenly seemed to find the floor fascinating. Even Richie, who'd brought the news, didn't look nearly as pleased as she expected. Her mother, Serafina, wore an expression that could only be described as ... resigned.

"What's going on?" Angie demanded, her happiness dimming like a candle caught in a draft.

"Nothing," Richie said too quickly. "I'm just delivering the news."

Angie turned to her mother, her suspicion rising. "I know you made other arrangements—a backup—when it seemed La Belle Maison wouldn't work out. But now, if it's possible to have the caterer you lined up deliver to the Maison instead, I'm sure the guests wouldn't mind a short delay with dinner. It'll be fine."

Serafina hesitated, her gaze darting toward her other daughters before returning to Angie. She lifted her chin, voice calm and carefully neutral. "Of course. We can manage. We know you have your heart set on that place."

Something in the way she said "that place"—as though La Belle Maison were no more than an inconvenience—made Angie freeze. Her pulse quickened. Slowly, she looked from her mother to her sisters, then to Richie, whose crestfallen expression spoke volumes.

"Wait," she said, her voice unsteady. "You never told me exactly what your back-up plan was. And right now, I can see you all rather liked that plan." Her chest tightened as the thought took shape in her mind, her voice hushed, almost fearful. "Are you saying … you liked your other plan better than La Belle Maison?"

The silence in the room was thick.

"It's all right," Serafina insisted, though her voice carried more steel than comfort. She cut a sharp glance at everyone else, silencing them with a matriarch's authority. "We all know what you've got your heart set on."

"That's right," Bianca, the peacemaker in the family, nodded her agreement to Serafina's words.

"Oh, for pity's sake," Connie burst out, unable to stand the charade any longer. "Tell her! Angie, they came up with a great idea—more than great—but they know it isn't the elegant well-known wedding venue you had your heart set on. But I think you should hear what their plan was before they change it."

Angie's throat tightened as her mind swirled. What could possibly be better than La Belle Maison? Still, she needed to be fair. She nodded to Connie. "I agree. I want to hear it. Mamma? Sisters? Someone—please, who's going to tell me?"

At last, Serafina sighed, resigned. "All right. I will." She squared her shoulders, regal as ever. "You know we tried to find a replacement venue when the Maison was closed, but every decent place was already booked. Then I thought—why look elsewhere when we have a wonderful place in the family? Richie's club. Big Caesar's. It has everything—a ballroom, a bandstand, liquor, even a kitchen. But it was already reserved tonight for a big, fancy fundraiser."

Richie shifted uncomfortably as Serafina pressed on. "So I spoke to the man in charge. I offered him a donation, a very large donation, in exchange for moving the event to another date. He agreed. The Children's Hospital fundraiser will be held next month instead, which actually works better for them. Of course, he did not turn down the donation. It's tax-deductible, which made your father almost smile." Her eyes softened as she added, "And Richie isn't charging us a penny—not for the club, the staff, or even the wine."

Angie's eyes darted to Richie. He gave a sheepish shrug and nodded.

But her mother wasn't done. "Then, there was the food. I do not like catered food, Angelina. You know this. It's never as good as home cooking. So I called your sisters, your cousins, a few close friends. We all spent last night, after the rehearsal dinner, in the kitchen. Everyone made their best dishes, their most special recipes, for your wedding. And we brought them all to the night club's kitchen at noon today to be there and ready for the reception. So, no, we don't have a fancy caterer, we just have ourselves and our food. It's family food." Her voice wavered with pride. "We even hired extra helpers so Richie's staff wouldn't be overwhelmed. Everything was ready."

Angie's mouth fell open.

Bianca stepped in gently, her voice trembling but proud. "This morning, we went to Big Caesar's. Connie oversaw the decorating. We dressed it in white and rose, everything draped and glowing like a ballroom in a fairy tale. Angie, it looks like Cinderella's ball. That was our surprise for you. But now—" she glanced toward Richie, then to her mother, her own smile faltering—"it seems you don't need it."

By the time Bianca finished, a lump rose so thick in Angie's throat she could barely speak. She turned in a circle, looking at them all—her mother, her sisters, her cousin, even the little boy in the corner. Their faces were a strange mix of pride, hope, and disappointment, as though they'd lost something they'd worked tirelessly to give her.

"All of you … you did all that for Paavo and me?"

Serafina straightened her back, her voice firm though her eyes glistened. "We had to have a place to dance at your wedding, Angelina. Nothing less would do."

Angie turned to Richie. "And you gave up your club on a Saturday night? Your busiest night of the week?"

Richie smiled, though his eyes were glassy with emotion. "What else would I do for my fav—" he glanced around at her sisters as well as his cousin Gina, mother of the flower girl, and corrected himself with a lopsided grin—"one of my favorite cousins?"

That was it. Tears began to spill from Angie's eyes despite her frantic attempts not to ruin her makeup. "Thank you so much, Mamma"—Angie hugged Serafina—"and Richie"—she put her arms around her cousin—"and everyone else. Forget the stuffy old La Belle Maison. What was I even thinking?" She laughed through her tears. "We're going to Big Caesar's—for the best, most beautiful reception San Francisco has ever seen."

CHAPTER 25

Saturday, 3 p.m. – the time of the wedding

Angie's heart pounded so hard she thought she might faint. For the first time in her life, she truly understood why a bride was not expected to make the walk down the aisle alone. A father's arm, a steadying hand—it wasn't just tradition. It was salvation.

The church was hushed now, guests already seated. Somewhere at the front, Paavo and his groomsmen waited. Just the thought of him standing there—tall, steady, and hers—made her breath catch in her throat. She tried to picture him, but her mind spun so fast she could barely hold an image.

Connie bent over her, fussing with the hem of her gown and the fall of her veil.

"Perfect," Biana whispered, and then nodded toward the church assistant. A moment later, the doors swung open and the first notes of Wagner's *Bridal Chorus* rolled through the air.

That was when Angie nearly lost it.

Yes, it was the traditional "Here Comes the Bride," the same march everyone said was tired, predictable, even boring. But to Angie, it was everything. She had dreamed of this music since she was a little girl playing dress-up in her mother's lace curtains. Her mother had walked to it, her sisters, her cousins—it was the music of Amalfi brides. As it swelled around her now, her heart felt so full she thought it might burst.

The bridesmaids, Bianca and Caterina, side-by-side entered first, followed by Maria and Francesca. Angie was surprised they could walk so steadily and look so graceful. She didn't think she could manage a step. Next, Connie, as matron-of-honor and looking radiant walked alone, carrying herself as if this wedding were her own. Micky, solemn as a little judge, marched down the aisle with the rings, while Michaela scampered behind, scattering rose petals in a trail of pink and white.

Then it was Angie's turn.

She lifted her chin, braced her shoulders, and slipped a trembling hand onto her father's arm. Salvatore Amalfi—tall and straight despite his gauntness, his olive skin and proud nose a mirror of her heritage—looked at her with such love that for a moment she thought she might collapse against him. He smiled, and that smile gave her strength.

They stepped forward together.

The church filled with gasps, with whispers of delight. Heads turned, bodies leaned into the aisle, and the oohs and aahs swelled like a tide. But Angie hardly noticed. She saw only Paavo.

There he stood at the altar, waiting.

Her breath caught. He was devastatingly handsome in his black tuxedo, broad-shouldered and steady, his pale blue eyes locked on hers as though no one else existed in the world. Behind him were Yosh, Doc Griggs, Richie, Bo Benson, and Luis Calderon, all lined up in their formal suits, but Angie barely registered them. The altar was draped in flowers, the priest and deacon both solemn in their traditional and colorful vestments, but still—her gaze never wavered.

Every step she took toward him was both impossible and inevitable. She smiled as she passed faces in the pews, but she couldn't have said who they belonged to. All she knew was that Paavo was there, waiting for her, and that each step brought her closer to the rest of her life.

At last, her father placed her hand in Paavo's, and she felt the warmth of his strong fingers closing over hers. Salvatore's eyes glistened as he stepped back, and Angie knew what it had cost him to let her go. Connie whisked away the bouquet, and suddenly Angie was standing side by side with the man she loved beyond measure, listening as the priest's voice rose above the music of her heart.

The ceremony unfolded in a blur of words and ritual, just as it was supposed to. No one jumped up to object to the wedding. No phones rang. No SWAT team descended on them. Not even a minor earthquake. For once, no disaster swooped down out of the blue to ruin the moment. The universe, it seemed, had finally granted them this one perfect hour.

As they said their vows, Paavo's voice was steady, though she saw the glint of emotion in his eyes. He spoke each word as though it were sacred, binding, and unshakable. He did not falter, did not joke, did not even call her his "waffle-wedded wife" as he'd once threatened to do after hearing about one tongue-tied groom saying just that. He simply vowed himself to her, wholly, completely, and forever.

She had promised herself when the time came for her vows, she wouldn't let a single tear fall, that she would get the words out clearly, but the sight of him—the sound of his voice, the weight of what they had endured to get here—made her throat ache. Somehow, she managed to speak and pledge herself to him with all the love in her heart.

When the priest pronounced them husband and wife, Paavo lifted her veil and kissed her.

In that instant, Angie's whole world shifted. Joy rushed through her like sunlight breaking over storm clouds. Her eyes filled and her heart swelled with the feeling of pure, unshakable happiness.

The rafters shook with Mendelssohn's *Wedding March,* the triumphant chords ringing like bells inside her very bones. Connie returned her bouquet to her left hand, Paavo's fingers tightened around her right. And together they turned and hurried down the aisle as husband and wife.

The guests rose, the music thundered, and petals floated like confetti around them. Angie laughed through her tears, unable to hold them in any longer.

After everything—the danger, the heartbreaks, the mysteries solved and the risks survived—finally, they were married.

CHAPTER 26

Angie's too-weepy eyes wanted to mist over again the moment she stepped into Richie's nightclub.

Big Caesar's had always been a lovely place, but tonight it was transformed into something beyond magical. Nestled in North Beach, close to Fisherman's Wharf, the club was known for its retro elegance: white-cloth tables circling a gleaming dance floor, the air always buzzing with jazz and swing. Normally, it was the kind of place where couples came dressed to impress, sipping cocktails under soft lights, gliding to music from the thirties to today.

But tonight? Tonight, it was a white wonderland.

Every detail—ribbons, banners, gleaming napkins, and the towering cake displayed like a jewel at center stage—had been touched by Connie and her sisters. Angie's throat tightened. *They did this for Paavo and me.*

The Amalfi sisters had pulled off miracles before, but this one was breathtaking.

Already, the guests had discovered the bar and was reveling in the abundant spread: beer and house wines free, premium wines and cocktails at cost. There was laughter, clinking glasses, a hum of warmth and energy.

The guests were an interesting mixture of her relatives, family friends, friends from school, cooking classes, and various jobs she'd had over the years, mingled with people here for Paavo. She saw lots and lots of police—cops from the precinct where Paavo had worked before going to Homicide, and inspectors from different divisions, including CSI and even the Medical Examiner, as well as familiar faces from his youth—Doc Griggs, Lupe at his side, and Joonas Maki were there beside Aulis Kokkonen, all reminiscing with a sparkle in their eyes. Paavo had always seen himself as a loner. *He has more friends than he ever realized,* she thought, her heart swelling.

Richie, natural showman that he was, emceed the introductions, his voice booming and playful. Then Maria's husband, Dominic Klee, and his band took over. He announced it was time for the newlywed's first dance. Angie's breath hitched as she and Paavo walked to the center of the dance floor. The choice of song had been hers, and although she looked and listened to one song after the other, old, new, and in between, no song captured what the two of them had gone through as much as one particular song.

Everyone, from Paavo's co-workers, to her family and friends had given the couple their heartfelt advice—and every last one of them had warned against getting caught up in a love affair that simply could never work out, that could never last. But, despite what all these "wise men" and "wise women" said, she and Paavo couldn't fight what they felt for each other. So she ended up choosing one of the most often played wedding songs of all, but it was so right for them, she couldn't resist it.

Just as she could never resist him.

Maria's husband picked up the microphone as they stepped into each other's arms, and then his deep, crooning voice sang "Can't Help Falling in Love with You."

The meal that followed was a feast of a family's love. Long buffet tables groaned under trays of manicotti, cannelloni, roast pork, stuffed zucchini—family classics—and, in a sweet nod to Angie's friends from "Wings of an Angel," Butch's infamous "special" spaghetti sauce made its appearance. Angie whispered a prayer he wouldn't tell anyone his "secret ingredient," or the Italian Benevolent Association might stage a protest.

The food was plentiful, but more than that—it was *theirs*. Every bite carried love. Guests raved, laughed, and went back for seconds and thirds, and Angie could feel joy fill the room as tangibly as the scent of garlic and basil.

And then, Rebecca Mayfield arrived.

Angie blinked. The homicide inspector was almost unrecognizable. Instead of her usual pulled-back ponytail and no-nonsense wardrobe, she wore a shimmering emerald dress, her blonde hair flowed past her shoulders, and her blue eyes were radiant. Richie, predictably, spotted her instantly. With all the subtlety of a charging bull, he plowed his way across the room, nearly toppling a young man who'd hoped for her attention. Angie caught the way Rebecca's eyes lit—yes, lit—before she quickly looked away.

"Nothing going on," Richie had claimed. Angie smiled knowingly. *We'll see.* But at the same time, she felt a twinge of uneasiness for him. Did he have any inkling of what he was in for if he were to become serious about a homicide inspector? Not only her crazy hours and weariness when pursuing a difficult case, but the constant worry he'd have over the danger inherent in her going after murderers.

Angie drew in her breath, easing her concern by reminding herself that after Richie's fiancée had been killed in a traffic accident—a wonderful, sweet woman who had worked in a bank and had never done anything dangerous in her too-short life—he'd never been serious about any woman. Did he like being around them? Definitely. But serious? Not so much.

Maybe his interest in Rebecca would be as short-lived as everyone had hoped her interest would be in Paavo.

Dancing followed the meal, beginning with the traditional father-daughter dance. Angie's heart squeezed as Salvatore Amalfi, frail yet proud as ever, guided her across the floor to *The Way You Look Tonight*. Midway through, Paavo joined with Serafina, and soon there was a graceful switch—Sal and Serafina became partners as Paavo danced Angie over to his stepfather. She managed to coax Aulis Kokkonen onto the floor to finish the dance with her. At the same time, Paavo found Richie's mother, Carmela Amalfi, and led her onto the dance floor. She beamed at the honor and that she hadn't been forgotten. It was as though the entire family was weaving themselves together, stitch by stitch, with each turn of the music.

Time passed in a blur of laughter, music, and clinking glasses. Before long, almost everyone was dancing, or drinking, or eating the goodies that remained on the dessert table, despite knowing they had to leave room for cake.

As Angie and Paavo circulated to talk to the guests and thank them for coming, she heard nothing but praise about the food and location of the reception. She noticed, too, that Richie monopolized Rebecca's time on the dance floor as well as when she wasn't dancing, and that Rebecca seemed to be enjoying every minute with him.

Angie was talking to Connie when a man she hadn't seen for quite a while came up to them. She had tried hard to find him, and when she succeeded, she had sent him a thoughtful and personal invitation. He hadn't sent a response, and she hadn't expected him to show up. But he did.

"Max Squire," she said. Connie spun around, and her face brightened with surprise and something more. Connie had cared about Max, but when they met, he was going through a very difficult time, and nothing ever came of their mutual attraction. Angie hoped that enough time had passed that he might be ready to look at life anew, to make a fresh start.

"Thank you for coming, Max," Angie said. "I'm sure you and Connie have much to catch up on, so I'll leave you two alone."

Max could barely tear his eyes from Connie's but he managed to murmur "Congratulations," to Angie and to thank her for inviting him. He had gone to the wrong location, he said to explain his late arrival, but a sign was posted on the door directing people here. Angie nodded, glad to hear it. She found Paavo and pointed out Max. Paavo said "Good," and was about to add something more, when his face froze and he stiffened. "Excuse me," he murmured.

Alarmed, she followed his gaze.

A figure appeared at the edge of the dance floor. Angie stared, hardly daring to believe. Her eyes jumped to Paavo. His body stilled, his expression immobile, as though the world had stopped. Then, without a word, he moved forward.

And Angie understood.

The music shifted to an old ballad, *Unforgettable,* and Angie knew that was what this moment would always be for herself, for Paavo, and for the older woman whose hand he took.

He led the woman to the dance floor and put his arm around her. She held herself stiffly even as she put one hand on his shoulder, the other in his. Her skin was well tanned, her hair short and gray. She was tall and trim, her cream-colored dress simple, and her eyes locked on Paavo's with pride, with love, and with years of unspoken sorrow.

His mother.

They moved together slowly, no words passing, just that gaze, as if both wanted, needed, this time together to last as long as possible. Angie stood watching, her own emotions all but painful as she watched the tenderness of this moment. Before the song ended, Paavo stopped dancing and said something to her. His mother nodded. He gently placed his hand on her waist and escorted her from the dance floor to Aulis Kokkonen and Jonas Maki. The old friends hugged and kissed and it seemed all of them shed a few tears—perhaps, Angie thought, to the memory of Paavo's father, a good and idealistic young man who had been taken from this world much, much too early.

But soon, Paavo escorted his mother toward the hall where he knew there were rooms where they could be alone and talk —to share a few moments of privacy, just the two of them.

So few people here would realize what they were seeing, what this moment meant. To everyone else, she might have been a stranger Paavo had once helped. But Angie knew. And she would never forget. She turned away, blinking hard. She prayed their time would be long, though she knew it could never be long enough.

She was still standing alone, grateful for Paavo having this moment, when Richie grabbed her hand and pulled her to the middle of the dance floor. "Now what?" she asked. A few people stopped what they were doing to watch.

Rebecca Mayfield smiled broadly at them.

Richie took off his jacket and a friend grabbed it. Then he took off his necktie and tossed it to one of Angie's old high school girlfriends standing nearby. She winked and smiled as she caught it. "Friends," Angie said to their quickly growing audience. "I have not asked him to do a striptease!"

Laughter, hoots, and catcalls sounded. He unbuttoned the top button of his shirt, then unbuttoned its cuffs.

"Richie," Angie loudly announced, by now understanding exactly what he was up to, "let me remind you, this reception is full of cops!"

"Come on, Angie," he said. "We've always danced this at other weddings. Let's show them how it's done," he said, and put both hands on his hips.

She laughed; then, put her hands on her hips.

With that, the band started playing the "Tarantella," the classic, ageless southern Italian folk music.

The two went into the lively dance, with its simple steps followed by raising their arms high and giving a clap in time with the music. They clasped each other's waist and danced in a circle, before breaking apart to again go into twirling steps, hands on hips, as the fun and flirtatious song was played. Soon, Richie got his mother to come onto the floor to dance with them, then Serafina, Angie's sisters, and before they knew it, most of the other Italians were joining in.

The tarantella broke the ice, and other men soon followed Richie's lead, removed their own jackets and ties, and headed for the dance floor. Young and old, cops and "civilians" were having fun, and mixed with each other, which was something that Angie, an acknowledged people-watcher, hadn't expected. It was obvious that more than a few of her girlfriends also had a thing for a guy in a uniform even if his uniform was currently at home.

Richie had the band strike up another old Italian favorite, "C'e la Luna Mezz'o Mare." Only when Angie got older and understood what was being said did she realize why everyone would laugh so uproariously when anyone sang the song about the young woman who desperately wanted to get married. She'd tell her mother about each of her suitors, and the mother would have some choice comments—filled with double entendres—as to why they were "unsuitable"until she mentioned the butcher boy. That one the mother approved of ... because he'd have a lot of "meat."

Angie was surprised at how well Dominic sang that song—

Maria had taught him well—and he had everyone who understood his words all but rolling on the dance floor at his expressions.

Even Paavo, reentering the room, paused to watch her dance, his smile wide and boyish. He looked happy—truly happy—and that was all Angie needed.

The time then came for Yosh to make his toast before the cake was cut. Everyone sat, champagne glasses filled and ready, as Paavo's partner stood.

"It's my honor to toast Angie and Paavo on the day of their wedding," Yosh began. "I've been lucky enough to work with Paavo for some time now, and a better, truer partner no one could ask for. He's always had my back, and I've always tried my best to have his. We all know about his background, how much of a loner he was through most of his life, and how much Aulis Kokkonen meant to him throughout all those years—Aulis was the rock he needed to grow into the man he became."

Yosh paused as people applauded Paavo's step-father, then continued. "But Paavo was still alone, until one day, he met a very pretty, very *rich* young woman who someone wanted dead. Paavo managed to keep her alive, and to his—and everyone else's shock—that little bit of a woman actually managed to save his life, as well.

"As much as he tried to leave her after that, all of us knew he didn't really want to go. His struggles should go down in the annals of Homicide. And when he finally decided to propose and give her the ring, he set up one 'event' after the other, only to have them blow up in his face. We expected he'd come to work one morning and announce he'd hog-tied her and she finally said yes."

There were nods and chuckles from everyone in homicide at those words. Then Yosh continued. "Most best man's toasts have funny stories about the groom, but unfortunately, in our line of work, not much humorous happens … unless you're talking about the time Angie sent Homicide coffee and sandwiches, only the coffee was strawberry flavored, the sandwiches were little heart-shaped things filled with watercress or liver pâté, and *nobody wanted to tell Paavo* what we thought of his fiancée's taste." Chuckles and groans ensued. "But then, he took one bite of the liver and tossed it in the trash."

"What!" Angie cried in shock, staring at Paavo.

"Then," Yosh said, "there was also the time she hired a singer to serenade him, but the guy turned up at a crime scene to loudly sing 'O Sole Mio' … to the corpse, I guess. We never could quite figure that one out." Everyone laughed hard at that.

Yosh lifted his glass to the couple, and the guests stood and did the same. "It's been quite a ride, partner. And I know that your life, with Angie, will be even better. Congratulations to you both."

Next, the cake cutting ceremony began with lots of picture-taking, jokes, and well wishes. After the cake was cut and eaten while a few more songs played, Angie's Big Day was almost over. She only had to toss her bouquet, and then she and Paavo would leave the festivities to everyone else as they drove off to start their honeymoon and their life together.

"Are you ready?" Connie asked. Angie had noticed that ever since Max Squire entered the reception, Connie had scarcely left his side, other than to get Stan Bonnette some Tums when he was in pain from having over-eaten. "I am," Angie said, and Connie handed her the bouquet. Quickly, all the single girls stood in front of her as she went up onto the stage.

Angie saw Connie standing at the right-most edge, at the very back. It was going to be a long toss, but she could do it. "Is everyone ready to see who'll be the next bride?" she asked.

As the group roared "Yes!" she turned her back to them, and with a mighty heave, sent her bouquet way up into the air, and then quickly turned around to see if she had aimed correctly.

All the hands were outstretched, and Angie watched in horror as one woman leaped to grab the bouquet as it sailed directly towards Connie. But the woman's timing as well as her catching ability were off, so her hands were still going upward when the bouquet passed overhead, causing her fingertips to hit the flowery missile, making it bounce upward yet again.

Connie's face showed her dismay as the treasured orb flew over her head and sailed directly toward, of all people, Cousin Richie. He looked absolutely horrified as the flying flowers catapulted towards him. He ducked.

Rebecca had been behind him, clearly wanting nothing to do with bouquets or weddings. Out of pure reflex and self-preservation, she tried to take a big step backwards, but in a tight dress and high heels instead of her usual slacks and boots, she wobbled and her arms raised up in an attempt to keep her balance. The bouquet landed snuggly within them. She stood open mouthed, gaping at it as if it were some mysterious creature from another planet as everyone clapped and cheered.

Richie righted himself, looking every bit as stunned as Rebecca.

Then, for some reason both of them turned to the other. Rebecca's eyes widened; Richie stared at her without blinking, and then both did an about-face and hurried off in opposite directions. As Paavo helped Angie from the stage, they exchanged a look, then burst into laughter.

"It's time for us to be on our way," Angie said as she took his arm and leaned close, filled with joy to be soon leaving the reception and to be alone with her new husband. "But something tells me another story may be just beginning."

Paavo turned her away from the crowd so that they only saw each other. "If so, may their days be filled with love and joy the way mine have been from the time we met. I love you, Miss Amalfi, even if I won't be calling you that anymore. And I always will."

She stepped closer to him. "And I love you, Inspector Smith. Forever."

With that, he kissed her. And that sealed the perfect ending to her perfect Big Day.

The End

ABOUT THE AUTHOR

Joanne Pence was born and raised in northern California and now lives in Idaho. She has been an award-winning, *USA Today* best-selling author of mysteries for many years, but she has also written historical fiction, contemporary romance, romantic suspense, a fantasy, and supernatural suspense. All of her books are now available as ebooks and in print, and most are also offered in special large print editions. Joanne hopes you'll enjoy her books, which present a variety of times, places, and reading experiences, from mysterious to thrilling, emotional to lightly humorous, as well as powerful tales of times long past.

Visit her at www.joannepence.com and be sure to sign up for Joanne's mailing list to hear about new books.